"Do you thi
between the
curator an
Becca

Her mind spun with the incidents that had occurred over the past few months in Colorado Springs, all wrapped up in the Vance and Montgomery families, who had been instrumental in Escalante's downfall the year before.

When she thought of the drug lord being alive, she grew chilled. Once again she pictured Quinn Montgomery, with his chocolate-brown eyes and a smile that could melt a woman's heart. He could take care of himself, but worry over his safety took hold and she couldn't shake off her concern. Someone had tried to burn his business down and had nearly succeeded. What if he'd been in the shop when it had been set on fire?

* * *

FAITH AT THE CROSSROADS: Can faith and love sustain two families against a diabolical enemy?

Books by Margaret Daley

MARGARET DALEY

feels she has been blessed. She has been married more than thirty years to her husband, Mike, whom she met in college. He is a terrific support and her best friend. They have one son, Shaun.

Margaret has been writing for many years and loves to tell a story. When she was a little girl, she would play with her dolls and make up stories about their lives. Now she writes these stories down. She especially enjoys weaving stories about families and how faith in God can sustain a person when things get tough. When she isn't writing, she is fortunate to be a teacher for students with special needs. Margaret has taught for over twenty years and loves working with her students. She has also been a Special Olympics coach and participated in many sports with her students.

Hearts
On The Line

Margaret Daley

Steeple
Hill®

Published by Steeple Hill Books™

Special thanks and acknowledgment are given to Margaret Daley for
her contribution to the FAITH at the CROSSROADS miniseries.

To Therese, Vickie, Jan, Caron and Gloria
Thank you for all your support and friendship.

To Captain Carole Newell
Thank you for all your help in researching what
a hostage negotiator does.

STEEPLE HILL BOOKS

Steeple
Hill ®

ISBN 0-373-87371-9

HEARTS ON THE LINE

Copyright © 2006 by Harlequin Books S.A.

www.SteepleHill.com

Printed in U.S.A.

Behold, God is my salvation; I will trust, and not be afraid; for the Lord Jehovah is my strength and my song; He also has become my salvation.

—*Isaiah* 12:2

CAST OF CHARACTERS

Quinn Montgomery—The target of vandalism and arson, the head of Montgomery Construction was ready for a break from all the tension. But with a madman on the loose gunning for the entire Montgomery clan, Quinn needed his faith to get him through….

Rebecca Hilliard—The Colorado Springs police detective had been busy for months investigating the various crimes perpetrated against the Vance and Montgomery families. Was she too busy for romance with Quinn?

Baltasar Escalante—The drug lord was hiding out in Colorado Springs with a new face, plotting to take back his only living heir. He'd vowed to destroy his hated enemies for taking his son away from him…but would he succeed?

Ritchie Stark—The small-time criminal had moved himself up in the crime world. Was he El Jefe, the brains behind the drug operation, or was he just a small fish in a large, deadly pond?

PROLOGUE

"Did anyone follow you?" Baltasar Escalante stepped out from the shadows cast by the pine trees.

Dahlia Sainsbury came to a halt on the trail path, feeling out of place in high heels and a pale-blue silk suit, but then she hadn't had time to change since leaving her office, having spent the past few days trying to convince the police she knew nothing about the drugs being moved beneath the museum. "No, I made sure before turning into the park." She smoothed a few strands of her hair that had come loose from her chignon.

Pausing in front of Baltasar, she scanned the area, half expecting the police to surround them after the incident with Alessandro and Colleen in the mine tunnels. "We can still leave for England, especially now that the authorities know about your involvement with the drugs." Her time in Colorado Springs was coming to an end. A little more time to cover her tracks and set a trap for Escalante, then she would be gone.

"I am not leaving until I've finished what I came here for."

The steel thread woven through his words sent a shiver down Dahlia. In the nearly full moon she saw his whipcord body stiffen, his hands fisted at his sides. "They know you're behind everything that's happening in Colorado Springs. Every police officer in the city is looking for you. Is the revenge worth getting caught?" She knew his answer even before he said anything because it was the same as hers. He would pay for having her half brother killed. They were alike in a lot of ways.

"I will not get caught. I have a place to hide out until I carry out the rest of my plans because, my dear, revenge is sweet. The Vances and Montgomerys will pay for destroying my life. They will suffer as I have."

She couldn't help the chill that rippled through her again.

"Cold, *querida?*" Escalante moved into her personal space, drawing her into his embrace.

The wind picked up and teased the few stray strands of her hair. "Just worried about you," she said in a voice filled with sincerity. She was getting good at lying. She agreed revenge would be sweet once *he* was dead.

Tilting up her chin, Escalante looked into her eyes as though delving beneath the surface to discover the true person behind the facade she presented. He dipped his head forward and brushed his lips across hers. She suppressed the shudder and tried to return his kiss with the feelings expected of a lover. But his cold kiss left her chilled.

Baltasar shifted. Something pressed into her chest. Then he backed away a few paces. In the moonlight

Dahlia saw the gun in his hand. A gun pointed at her heart.

She couldn't take her eyes off the weapon. "Why?"

"You are Alistair Barclay's sister. Did you think I wouldn't find out? I wanted to double-cross you first."

The icy declaration sealed her fate. She whirled to run. A deafening sound pierced the air at the same time as the force of the bullet propelled her forward. She went down on her knees. Pain gripped her as blackness hovered….

ONE

On the path, Detective Becca Hilliard paused for a second, taking in her surroundings at the Garden of the Gods Park. As she approached a crime scene, she liked to get her bearings, especially when it was outside.

The metallic stench of blood laced the cool morning air. A pale-blue sky with a few streaks of white stretched out above her. The soaring red rock formations in the park and Pikes Peak jutting upward in the background vied for her attention. The day was beautiful. Too beautiful for a murder, but since being transferred to homicide, she had learned a murder could happen anywhere, anytime.

A few uniforms stationed around the perimeter of the crime scene and, off to the side, a young couple with her partner, Sam Vance, were the only people in this more isolated area of the park. The man had his arm around the woman, trying to comfort her. Sam spoke to the blond lady whose pale, tear-streaked face brought forth all the churning emotions Becca experienced when viewing a violent crime. She wasn't sure she would ever be able to anesthetize herself completely when seeing a dead body, as some of her fellow police officers had managed to do.

Sam gave her a nod and headed toward her. "We gotta stop meeting like this."

"I wish."

"It's Dahlia Sainsbury, the curator at the Colorado Springs Impressionist Museum. With all that has happened lately, I can't say that I'm surprised by this murder."

"Especially since she's suspected of a connection to the drugs that were being distributed from the tunnels under the museum. Alessandro was sure she knew what was going on. He believes that she tried to poison Colleen. It would have only been a matter of time before we had enough evidence to formally charge her."

"Yeah, she was playing with the big boys, and they don't play fair."

"Do you think Escalante killed her because of what happened in the tunnels with Alessandro? If so, why?" Becca gestured toward the face-down body of Dahlia, a bullet hole in her back, red fanning out from it. Becca's gaze riveted to the dead woman's left arm, which was stretched out above her head. "It certainly wasn't robbery. That diamond bracelet on her arm has to be worth a small fortune. And her purse is next to her."

"With everything in it, as far as we can tell. It clearly wasn't robbery. She was shot at very close range."

"Which means she either was surprised or knew the person who shot her and was running away. How long has she been dead?"

"With lividity and rigor mortis, the medical examiner says between six and ten hours. He'll know more after he examines the body at the morgue."

"So what was Dahlia Sainsbury doing in the park after hours?"

"Meeting someone? We found a set of footprints near the body. A man's, from the size."

Becca stepped closer to the body and examined it, making sure not to disturb any evidence since the crime-scene unit hadn't arrived yet. "It doesn't look like there was much of a struggle. Who found her? That couple?"

"Yeah, I've got some uniforms canvassing the area to see if anyone else heard something, but I doubt it with this place's isolation."

"Let's separate our couple. You take the man. I'll take the woman." Becca made her way toward the pair.

The blonde raised her head, her teary gaze taking in Becca's approach.

"Hello, I'm Detective Becca Hilliard. May I have a word with you?" She placed her hand on the woman's arm and directed her to the side, away from the young man. Reaching into her jacket pocket of her navy blue pantsuit, she retrieved her pad and pen then continued, "I'm so sorry you had to find this. It's never easy, Ms....?"

"Carrie Young," the woman said with a sniffle, brushing her hand across her cheek.

"Is that your boyfriend? Husband?"

Carrie glanced at the man talking to Sam. "Just a good friend. We like to hike together. This was our favorite trail until—" She hugged her arms to herself, her eyelids sliding closed for a few seconds while she sucked gulps of air into her lungs.

"Tell me what happened." Even after eight years on the force, Becca had a hard time dealing with the effects that a death caused on the people left behind. Interviewing the person who found a body or a loved one of the victim drained her emotionally.

"There isn't much to tell. We were walking along the trail. She isn't hard to see. She's—she's—" Carrie swallowed several times "—right there two feet from the path." She waved her hand in the direction of the body but didn't look at it, her mouth compressed into a frown.

"Did you touch her or anything?"

Carrie's eyes grew round. "Me? No! I couldn't. Bud did, though. He checked for a pulse to see if she was alive."

"Where?"

"On her neck. He said she was cold." Carrie shuddered, clasping her arms even tighter to her. "I had my cell phone. I called the police. We waited for them at the trail head. I couldn't wait here." Another tremor shook the woman.

"Can you think of anything else?"

"She wasn't dressed for hiking or the outdoors. She looks like she was dressed for a date."

Becca remembered the spiked blue heels and matching silk dress that Dahlia wore and had to agree with Carrie. Who had she been dating? Becca jotted a note to herself to check into that. Maybe this wasn't connected to the drug gang, Escalante and everything else that had happened in the past few months, starting with the attempted murder of the mayor. First rule of police work: don't assume anything.

The ring on Becca's cell phone blared "Old Mac-Donald Had a Farm." She unhooked it from her waist and flipped it open. "Hilliard here."

"A man's threatening to jump off the new building going up at Carson and Quincy."

"I can be there in fifteen." She clipped the phone back on her belt and said to Carrie, "I have to leave. My partner will take the rest of your statement." She quickly moved to Sam. "Can you finish? That was Sarge. I've got a jumper."

"Sure," Sam said as she started down the trail at a jog.

Two minutes later, as the crime-scene unit pulled into the parking lot, Becca peeled out, siren on, and raced toward the construction site, hoping she could make it before the person carried through with his threat. As a member of the negotiation team for the police department, she responded to hostage, suicide or barricade situations when the need arose. Her heart raced, with adrenaline pumping into her system as fast as her car sped toward her destination.

Becca drove to the cordoned-off area where the team leader had set up his command post. Beyond the barricade a crowd of people gathered with their attention glued to the top of the unfinished building. Leaping from her car, she went to her trunk and removed her body armor. The man threatening suicide stood on the top ledge ten stories up. Most likely he didn't have a gun, but she never knew, so she always wore protection.

"What do we have, Sarge?" Becca asked the team leader, Carl Johnson, as she slipped on her body armor.

"I just got here myself a few minutes ago. Quinn Montgomery called 911 and is talking to the man right now. He's the man's boss, owns the company putting up this building. The first person on the scene was a uniform. He's up there now with Montgomery."

"Who's the jumper?"

"David James. Don't know much yet. Here, put this transmitter on." Sarge handed her a beeperlike device to clip at her waist. "And use this earpiece. I'll feed you information on the jumper as I get it."

She rode the elevator to the top floor and hurried toward the stairs that led to the roof, nodding toward the uniformed officer standing guard at the door. Wind played with stray strands of her ponytail. The sun beat down, heating the concrete. She'd prefer to wear her sunglasses, but it was important for David James to see her eyes and connect with her. Instead, she squinted against the glare and headed toward a large man standing a few feet from the jumper, who was poised on the ledge. One step the wrong way and David would go down ten stories.

"David, I'll help you any way I can. Just come down from there."

Montgomery's deep, baritone voice held a calm, soothing tone. Becca was impressed that even his stance didn't convey any irritation or anger. She placed her hand on Montgomery's arm to indicate she was present since his full attention was on his employee. He gave her a slight nod but kept his gaze trained on the jumper.

David glanced her way. His eyes widened. He took a small step to the side away from her and Montgomery, but didn't say anything.

"Hello, David. I'm Becca Hilliard. I'm a negotiator with the police. I'd like to help you."

"Help me? No one can!"

Becca moved next to Montgomery, aware that his gaze was now on her. The air sizzled with tension. "You don't think anyone can help you?"

David's attention darted to Montgomery then back to her. "My wife left me and took the kids. Can you bring her back and make everything like it was before—" He worked his mouth but no more words came out. Peering away, he clenched his hands at his sides.

Montgomery started to take a step toward David. Becca stopped him and shook her head. She mouthed the words, "Too dangerous."

David looked at her again. "I want things back the way they were."

"You sound frustrated."

"I am. There was no warning. I came home yesterday and she was gone." Anger lining his face, the jumper snapped his fingers, the gesture making him wobble.

Becca held her breath, knowing if he lost his balance neither she nor Montgomery would be able to reach the man in time. David steadied himself, his eyes growing round as he glimpsed the ground ten stories below. That was a good sign. Perhaps David hadn't thought this suicide attempt completely through. In her earpiece Sarge told her he would see what he could discover about David's wife.

"Do you plan to commit suicide, David?" she asked, having learned it was important to establish that up front.

He blinked. Montgomery stiffened beside her.

"I—I—don't—" David cleared his throat. "Yes. I don't have anything to live for. My family's gone. I have bills I can't pay."

Becca started to push Montgomery back toward the stairs, where it was safer, when he interjected, "I'll help you with that, David."

The jumper's gaze swung to the man next to her. Surprised by the offer, she, too, wanted to look at Montgomery, but she didn't dare take her eyes off David James. Again she acknowledged the calm power behind Montgomery's words, as though he knew instinctively what to do in a situation like this.

"You see, there are ways to help you, David. If you come down from there, we can talk about it." Becca concentrated on keeping her voice even, nonthreatening.

For a long moment David didn't say anything, then he shook his head as though trying to rid his mind of some image. "Help? I've tried talking to her. She won't listen."

"When you tried to talk to your wife, she wouldn't listen?"

David slowly turned so he could face her, but he remained on the foot-wide ledge. "Yes. I left messages at her mother's all evening and this morning for her to call me. She didn't! I was late to work because of her."

"Maybe she didn't get your messages."

Surprise flickered across his features. "You might be

right! It would be just like her mother not to tell her about my calls. She hates me."

"Come down here and we can try again." Becca pulled out her cell phone, dangling it in front of him as though it were a prize he couldn't possibly resist.

David glanced at the ground to his left, then back at Becca. She held her breath, hoping he would follow her gentle command. Sometimes that worked, especially if he hadn't totally thought through committing suicide.

David shrugged. "Okay."

Montgomery released a heavy sigh that mirrored her own feelings as she watched David climb down from the ledge and walk toward her, holding his hand out for the cell phone.

As he neared her, she began heading toward the stairs to the tenth floor below, saying, "Do you want me to make the call?" She wanted to get him as far away from the ledge as possible.

"No, I will."

David came up beside her while Montgomery took the rear. After passing the phone to David, she threw a glance over her shoulder, wishing Montgomery was a police officer in case they ended up in a scuffle. She hated involving civilians. Montgomery smiled and nodded as though he could read her mind and was re-assuring her he could take care of himself. With his muscular build, no doubt he could, she decided, a con-nection arcing between her and Montgomery. They were both determined to keep David from jumping.

"Trish, pick up. This is David. I've got to talk to you. Please!"

Anger, mixed with frustration, returned to David's face. Becca slowly retrieved her handcuffs from her pocket and prepared for if he decided to dash for the ledge again. If she had her way, he wouldn't, now that she had him down from it.

He snapped the phone closed and cursed. "She's gonna regret not taking my call when—"

Before David had a chance to finish his sentence, Becca grabbed his arm and twisted first one, then the other, behind his back and locked the handcuffs on his wrists. David jerked around, obviously intending to head back up to the roof. Montgomery blocked David's path in the stairwell to the tenth floor. From behind, several uniformed officers rushed up and whisked the jumper away, as he screamed his frustration.

All the emotions and tension she had held at bay during the ordeal flooded Becca the minute she realized David wouldn't be jumping that day, that he might get the help he needed. While the uniform officers led him away, she sagged against the handrail, squeezing her eyes closed and drawing in cleansing breaths.

"Thank you."

Montgomery's deep voice penetrated the place she went in her mind where she tried to regroup after a negotiation. When she opened her eyes, he stood right in front of her, filling her vision, all six feet two inches of him. Now that she had the time to examine him, he took her breath away. Dressed in faded jeans and a short-sleeved blue shirt, he reinforced her earlier impression that he was all muscles and power. His chocolate brown eyes twinkled as the seconds ticked into a full minute and she hadn't said anything. A flush actually colored his cheeks.

"I'm sorry. I don't usually stare at people unless I think they're going to commit a crime. But after a negotiation, I'm wiped out, even when they don't last long, like this one."

The corner of his mouth cocked upward. "I think I know the feeling. I was so glad when you showed up." He plowed both hands through his short russet-colored hair, then scrubbed them down his face as though to wash the past hour from his mind. "I don't know how you do it. Are you called out much?"

"More than I wish. Usually a few times a month." She extended her hand. "Thank you for your help."

He took her hand within his and shook it. "I wasn't gonna let David jump."

His determination underscored her own in situations like this, and the connection she had felt earlier between them crackled again.

Still grasping her hand, he said, "But you don't have to worry about me applying for your job. One officer of the law in the family is enough for me."

The firmness and warmth in his touch conveyed the man she had heard about from his brother, Brendan, a former police officer who had until recently worked with her. She'd casually known Quinn Montgomery from afar, but suddenly there seemed nothing casual between them now.

"I miss Brendan at the CSPD, but he seems to be settling in at the FBI," Becca said, trying to dismiss the feeling of interest hovering below the surface.

"Yeah, he's a regular Elliot Ness."

"Not J. Edgar Hoover?" She started down the stairs, realizing that Sarge would be waiting for her.

"Nah, Brendan's more a hands-on type of guy, like me."

"Is that why you were here? Isn't Montgomery Construction a big operation?"

"I like to be involved in all the projects as much as possible, especially with what has happened lately."

"That's right. Wasn't there a fire at your business a few months back?"

"Yeah, my carpentry shop and storage barn were destroyed. A lot of things have been happening to the Montgomery family lately. It pays to keep an eye open. What's going to happen to David?" Quinn punched the down button for the elevator.

"He'll get the help he needs." She slanted a glance toward Quinn Montgomery, trying to remember all that Brendan had told her about his older brother. "Did you mean what you said about helping him with his bills?"

He nodded. "He'll need it."

"I've got a feeling David will appreciate it, especially when he straightens out his life." Now she remembered what Brendan had once said about his older brother. He was a man whose word was good as gold. She liked that.

Stepping onto the elevator, Quinn said, "I'm in your debt for showing up when you did. I didn't know how I was going to get him down from that ledge. I'd run out of ideas."

"You were doing a pretty good job of keeping him

calm. The important thing was that David was still there when I showed up."

That cocky smile reappeared. "I was afraid he could hear my knees knocking and the sound would drive him over the edge."

She laughed.

He liked the sound of her laughter—light, musical, as if it danced on the air. "Seriously, if I can do anything for you, return the favor in any way, please let me know."

"I was just doing my job, Mr. Montgomery."

"Quinn, and that doesn't mean I can't feel indebted to you for your assistance up on the roof, Becca. David was one of my employees, part of my family."

She turned her head toward him, her ponytail flying to one side with the sudden movement. That drew his attention to her light-brown hair, streaked with blond coloring. Her large hazel eyes focused on him, making him aware of the small confines in the elevator. For a moment his gaze connected with hers, and he became lost in her light-brown depths with green specks.

She blinked, stepping back a pace. "Thank you, but—"

The elevator doors whooshed open and the noise and activity rushed in to remind Quinn of what had just transpired for the past sixty minutes. What she was about to say to him was lost as a big man in a police uniform approached them.

"Becca, you did a good job." The man looked toward Quinn. "I'm the team leader, Carl Johnson. We'll need a statement from you, Mr. Montgomery."

"Fine. I'll come down to the station later today." After shaking Carl's hand, Quinn stepped to the side, seeing his younger brother coming toward him. "Again, thank you, Becca, for your help. If you need anything, let me know."

As Quinn walked away, he heard the man say to Becca, "We'll need your report while it's still fresh in your mind. This one ended good."

Quinn paused to watch Becca leave with her team leader and another police officer. Quinn still could picture her big eyes, full of life even in the midst of such turmoil and potential death. Her look reminded him of Maggie. The memory of the last time he'd seen Maggie pierced his heart. He shook the reflection from his mind. He had moved on. He wouldn't go down that path again.

"I hear you had some action this morning." Brendan patted him on the back. "And you handled yourself well."

"I told Becca Hilliard that she never has to worry about me applying for her job." Quinn walked toward the area where he had set up a makeshift office on site. Still fresh in his mind was the first few minutes up on the roof with David. Fear such as he rarely encountered had washed through him until he had said a prayer to God for guidance. Then, as though the Lord had clasped his shoulder and stood next to him, his fear had dissolved and in its place had been a resolve to see David safely down from the ledge. He had known that everything would be all right. Not long after that Becca Hilliard had arrived as though she had been sent from the Lord.

"You need to give a statement."

"I know. Just give me a few minutes. I need a strong cup of coffee and something sweet."

Brendan followed him into the room. "Pour me a cup, too."

"What brings you by?" Quinn handed his younger brother a mug full of hot, strong coffee, then filled a cup for himself.

"Heard about the jumper and came running. Couldn't see you going through this without me, especially with the trouble we've had lately. At first I thought it was connected to that."

"Nope. David James just lost it. His supervisor called him on being late for work. That sent the man over the edge. He flew at Collins, hit him a few times, then escaped up to the roof, where he threatened to jump."

"Is Collins okay?"

"Yeah, just a cut lip and probably a black eye." Quinn lifted his mug to take a sip and noticed his hand shaking. He placed the mug on his desk before he spilled his coffee. "How does she do it?"

"Who? What?"

"Becca. Negotiating." Quinn clasped his hands together to still their trembling, recognizing the reaction as delayed shock. When he had thought David would jump, all he could think of was the man's two little girls without their father. *Thank You, God, for delivering David safely down. And thank You for sending Becca to help.*

"Ah, now it's just Becca."

"Stop right there, little brother. After going through

something like what happened on that rooftop together, it seems kinda ridiculous to call the woman Ms. Hilliard."

Brendan lounged against the file cabinet. "She has her own methods of destressing. We all do."

Quinn knew his brother was referring to people working in law enforcement. He'd been engaged to a woman who had been on the police force until—again his heart twisted with the remembrance of that day Maggie had died. So much for not going down memory lane.

"You're the boss. Give yourself the rest of the day off. I think you deserve it."

"So I can go over what happened on the rooftop until I go screaming down the street? No, thank you. I think I'll stay and work." This was one of his ways of dealing with stress. Finally, Quinn thought his hand was steady enough to pick up his mug and take a long drink of his much-needed coffee. "How's Chloe? Have you two set a date yet?"

Brendan chuckled. "I get the picture. No more talking about you. Chloe and I are negotiating when. Definitely Chloe's the one."

"I'm glad, since you two are already engaged."

"How about you? Seeing anyone?"

"Don't have the time. The fire set me back some. Having to rebuild the shop and barn as well as do all the projects we're committed to has taken a lot of my extra time."

"I thought you finished the shop and barn a couple of weeks ago."

"Yes, but…" Quinn let his sentence trail off into the

silence. He and his brother knew the real reason he hadn't dated. Except for the few times Brendan had tried to fix him up since Maggie's death three years ago, he hadn't gone out with anyone. Instead, he had thrown himself into his work and his carpentry.

"She would have wanted you to move on, Quinn."

"I know. I am. Colleen has a friend at the paper she wants to introduce me to. I'm thinking about taking her up on her offer once she returns from Italy for her wedding."

The second Quinn said that, however, an image of Becca up on the rooftop, totally focused on David, calm and in control, popped into his mind. *There's something about Becca Hilliard that—no, don't go there. Her job is as dangerous as Maggie's was, and Maggie's job killed her.*

TWO

Becca took the stairs up to the attic and opened the windows at each end of it to let the cool breeze blow through and the stale air escape out. She had a few minutes before Quinn showed up and she wanted to find her sister's box of memorabilia to send to her. She'd been promising her for months, and if she didn't do it now, she would probably forget for another month—especially since her younger sister had just called asking her to send it to her.

Amazed that she still didn't have the time to do the things needed—after all, both her sister and brother no longer lived at home—Becca headed for the corner where Caitlin had kept her belongings. Her two siblings were gone, so why couldn't she find enough time to do all that needed to be done?

"Because I have now decided to finish my college degree in psychology on top of trying to solve the rash of recent murders. What did I expect?" she muttered to herself as she dug through the boxes for the one Caitlin had described. Being married to her job didn't allow a lot of extra time.

In the very back, perched on a rafter, she saw the black square box with her sister's treasures. Becca stretched over the containers piled in her way. Just a few more inches. She leaned farther forward, lost her balance and started to fall. With quick reflexes, she managed to catch herself by putting her hand down on the rafter while her foot came down hard in the area between two beams. The unfinished part of the floor held for a second, then suddenly her foot plunged down through it, the jagged edges of the wood ripping through her capri pants and digging into her thigh. Pain shot through her.

She swung her leg that dangled from the ceiling in the third bedroom on the second floor, hoping to give herself some momentum to shove herself up out of the hole she was caught in. She couldn't dislodge herself. She examined the area around her for something to use to drag herself out. Nothing. Frustrated, she slapped her hands on the two rafters, the only firm support around her, and pushed upward. Her leg, caught on something, wouldn't budge. Again, then again, she attempted to free herself as the pain continued to radiate up her leg.

Finally, in exhaustion she sagged against the wooden beam. Sweat dripped off her face and coated her white shirt. She took a moment to regain her strength while she ran through different scenarios in her mind. The only thing she could come up with was to keep trying and hope eventually sheer force would dislodge her.

The ringing of her doorbell cut into the sound of her heavy breathing. Quinn Montgomery. Maybe her knight in shining armor had arrived—not that she believed in such a thing. She'd learned earlier to depend on only herself and her work with the police department had only confirmed that through the eight years she had been on the force. But she was a practical person and right now she needed help.

The chimes sounded again.

"Quinn! Help!" she yelled, hoping he heard with the windows open. "Help!"

"Becca…" She heard his wonderful, deep voice calling up to her through the window. "Where are you?"

"In the attic. I fell through the floor and can't get out."

"How do I get in? Do you have a spare key outside somewhere?"

The very thought appalled her. Why make it easy for a robber to get into her house? She'd be the butt of jokes at the police station for weeks. "No. My neighbor on the left has one."

"Be right back."

Even though help was on the way, Becca gave it another try, hating the idea she was trapped in her house, helpless, depending on another for rescue. Still, all she managed to do was press the jagged pieces of wood into her flesh even more. She bit down hard. She hoped she wasn't bleeding all over her grandmother's quilt, which covered Caitlin's bed. Granny would roll over in her grave if she was.

Moments later footsteps pounded up the stairs to the attic. She inhaled in a deep, calming breath, and nearly choked on the dust she'd stirred up. She sneezed, releasing one hand to rub her nose. She must look a wreck with sweat-drenched clothes covered in the dust and dirt from the floor. So much for second impressions.

"Becca?"

Realizing the mound of boxes hid her from his view, she called out, "I'm over here."

Quinn peered over the stack and, with a sharp gaze, assessed the situation with a quick sweep. "Okay?"

"Except for being embarrassed for putting myself in this position, I'm fine."

Quinn hefted the boxes out of the way until he could kneel next to her, careful to keep his weight on the rafter he balanced himself on. The worry on his face touched her. For so long she had always been the one who had worried about others. She'd forgotten what it was like to have someone concerned for her.

"I'm adding this to the long list of projects that need to be done around here. This attic flooring needs to be completed." She patted the beam next to her. "I definitely don't want to be in this predicament again." This would now be number one on her least favorite things to happen to her, even before encountering snakes, which she had a healthy fear and respect for.

Quinn grinned. "Probably should be moved up to the top of your 'to do' list." He felt around the edges of the hole.

"I'm caught on something." She breathed in a whiff of his aftershave and for a few seconds the scent of pine filled her nostrils.

"I'm going below to see if I can push you up through the hole. Do you have a stepladder somewhere?"

"In the garage."

"I'll be right back. Hang on." He rose, chuckling. "No pun intended."

"Oh, I'm not going anywhere," she said with her own chuckle.

She was sure when she was free she would laugh about this and probably tell the guys down at work about this little adventure—well, maybe she wouldn't go that far. But right now all she wanted was to hide in the bathroom, wash off the dirt she'd picked up from the floor and change clothes. What a sight she must be! There was a part of her that was amazed she even cared, but she had felt a connection with Quinn the other day that had intrigued her.

In the past she'd had little time for a serious relationship with the opposite sex what with raising her siblings and trying to establish her career at the police department as well as go back to school to finish her degree. She only had another year of part-time college to earn her psychology degree, then she wanted to work on her master's. She couldn't see herself being a police detective forever, especially considering how hard it was for her emotionally to shake some cases. She wanted one day to be a counselor. That was why she had joined the negotiation team. That and—

So lost in thought, she gasped when she felt Quinn's hand on her ankle. The warmth in his fingers momentarily wiped from her mind the past half hour and all she could zoom in on was his touch.

"I see a piece of wood caught on your pants. I'm going to free you then push up. I may have to rip your pants some more."

"I imagine they are beyond repair. Don't worry about them," she said wistfully when she thought of having just removed the price tag from them right before she had put them on an hour ago.

Quinn clambered up the ladder until he could grip the wood. The whole time she was acutely aware of him even though she couldn't see him—she could hear and feel his presence. Heat singed her face when she pictured how she must look to him.

He finally broke off the jagged piece of wood, giving her leg some more room. "Ready?"

"Yeah."

He shoved while she thrust herself up and out of the hole. She perched herself on the rafter and stared down into the bedroom. Thankfully she hadn't been right above the bed so Granny's quilt had escaped any harm.

"Are you all right?" Quinn's handsome face peered up at her.

She smiled. "I'll live."

He climbed down while she checked the gash on her leg. Her nicest pair of capris was, as she'd suspected, totally ruined. She probably needed to go to the doctor and have the wound stitched. Her leg throbbed with pain, which only reinforced her conclusion. She hated doctors, tried her best to stay away, but she knew Quinn would insist. Why, she wasn't sure. He just seemed that kind of guy.

Quinn appeared by her side. "How bad is it?"

She showed him the gash on her thigh, blood soaking her peach-colored capri pants.

He whistled. "I'll drive you to the emergency room."

"No hospitals."

"You should see a doctor. You need stitches and the wound needs to be cleaned out. I've seen enough accidents on the construction site to know a bad one when I see it."

Her jaw clenched, she tried to stand. "I don't have a doctor."

Quinn came to her side to assist. "You don't?"

She slanted a look at his strong profile as she limped next to him toward the stairs, his arm about her, helping to support some of her weight. "We had a family doctor, but he retired last year. I haven't had a need to find another."

"My cousin is a doctor. I'll call Adam and see if he can see you right away."

"But—"

He shot her a challenging look, one eyebrow arched.

She clamped her mouth closed, keeping her protest inside. Finally she said, "It's Saturday," as though that would change Quinn's mind.

"I'm calling him at home."

"I don't want to bother him at home on his—"

"That's what family is for. Family helps family."

Becca could tell by the firm set of his jaw and the intense look in his eyes that she wasn't going to get out of having Quinn take her to his cousin. And frankly, she didn't have a better option. Her leg throbbed and the deepness of the gash made it evident she needed help.

Downstairs in her kitchen where she kept her first-aid kit, she sat at her table, opened the container and retrieved a bandage and some peroxide. After calling his cousin, Quinn hovered over her, watching her every move as though if she fumbled he would step in to assist. In the short time she'd known him, she'd gotten that feeling about him. He was a man of action, no wasted motion.

"There. I shouldn't bleed all over your car." She snapped her first-aid kit closed.

Again with his assistance, she made her way to his blue truck, which was sitting in her driveway. "How far?" she asked, noticing a red spot on her bandage already.

Quinn glanced at her wound. "Ten minutes. Adam's meeting us at his office."

"This is probably not how you thought you would spend your morning."

He sent her a grin that caused her stomach to flip-flop. "After your leg is taken care of, we'll pick up where we left off."

"And that is?"

"With me ringing your doorbell and you answering. Oh, that reminds me—" he delved into the front pocket of his jeans and took out the key to her front door "—this is yours."

He slipped her house key into her palm, the action almost seeming intimate to Becca. Curling her fingers around the piece of metal, warmed by his touch, she shook that feeling away. When in the world would she have time to date, let alone get serious with someone? Her work took up so much of her day and what was left over was devoted to her classes and finally fixing up the home that should have been renovated years ago.

* * *

After having limped around her house for the past hour showing Quinn what needed to be done, in the living room Becca swept her arm wide and asked, "So, what do you think?"

He looked up from the pad he had been scribbling notes on and said, "Let me work up an estimate and get back to you."

"I know I can't afford all that needs to be done right away. I was thinking about having the work done in stages with the kitchen—" she glanced skyward "—and now the ceiling in the third bedroom and flooring in the attic done first."

"Okay, I'll start with that. I should have something by tomorrow afternoon. I can come by after church with the estimate. Will you be here around one?"

"That's my day to sleep in and be lazy, so I'll be here." Of course, her idea of sleeping in and being lazy was getting up at eight and actually getting to read the Sunday paper, then hitting the books for class, if she wasn't catching up on a few things that needed to be done around the house.

Contemplating her for a moment, Quinn cocked his head. "Why the kitchen?"

With her leg still throbbing, she decided to sit on the couch and indicated he take a seat, too. "Because I love to cook and hope to do more of it in the future."

"I do quite a bit of cooking when I have the time."

"You do?"

"Yeah, learned it from my mother."

She snapped her fingers. "That's right. I've had some

of your mother's apple pie at the Stagecoach Cafe. Brendan brought one down to the station a while back. It was delicious." Becca smoothed her hand across another pair of capris, thankful that she was finally able to take off the ruined ones, ripped beyond repair, which she'd promptly thrown away. "Any chance I could get her apple pie recipe?"

His chuckle spiced the air. "It's a deep, dark family secret. The only way is to become a member of the family."

The very thought sent her mind whirling with all kinds of possibilities, none unappealing. She tapped her finger against her chin and said, "Hmm. With Brendan engaged..."

His gaze caught hers and for a few seconds sparks flew across the short space that separated them. Then the moment evaporated when Quinn sat up and looked away, clearing his throat. "I'd better be going."

Reluctantly Becca pushed to her feet, part of her wanting to explore what had just transpired between them. But the other part wanted to run as fast as possible away from him. He could break her heart. She knew he had been engaged several years back and his fiancée, Maggie Nelson, a fellow police officer, had been killed while on duty. From the rumors flying around at the time, Quinn had not taken it well. Was he still mourning Maggie's death?

"I look forward to hearing from you about the estimate." She started for the entry hall. "And your cousin was great today. Are you sure he won't take some money for stitching me up?"

"Adam? No way! We Montgomerys help each other out."

"But I'm not a Montgomery."

"But I am and I asked him to help."

"So he's honor bound?"

"Yep. It's nice to have a doctor in the family."

The grin that spread across Quinn's face sent her heart beating a shade faster. When he opened the front door, his massive build dominated her entrance and for the strangest reason it seemed so right. "Thanks for all your help today."

"You're welcome. I'll call you tomorrow before coming over."

As she closed the door, she felt another strange sensation as though she were back in high school waiting for a call from a boy that never came. Instead, her life had been thrown into turmoil with her father being held hostage at the bank he worked at. Twenty-four hours later he had been killed by the gunman and she had become the strong one in her family. Her mother had fallen apart, unable to deal with two young children, ages eight and eleven. A year later her mother had gotten cancer, which had taken her life after a two-year battle with the disease.

The phone blaring startled Becca from her memories. She pushed away from the door and limped toward the kitchen, where she picked up the receiver on the fourth ring. "Hello."

"Becca, I'm turning down your street. I've got a lead on the O'Brien case."

Sam's statement completely anchored her in the present. "I'll be out front."

Quickly she located her purse and gun, then hurried as fast as she could out onto her porch and down the steps. Sam came to a stop in front of her house. She tried not to favor her injured leg, but she wasn't totally success-ful.

"What happened?" Sam asked as he pulled away from the curb.

"You know the statistics about most injuries happen-ing in the home? I'm living proof they're right. I fell through the floor in my attic."

Surprise widened Sam's eyes. "All the way?"

"No, just one leg, but I have a long gash in my thigh to remind me not to hurry when I'm doing something." She shifted to make herself comfortable. "So what's your lead?"

"Eddie Stinson was caught robbing a convenience store this week, and guess what? He used the same gun that killed Neil O'Brien. The ballistics report I just read confirmed it."

"So he's the killer?"

"No, he's got an airtight alibi. He was in jail at the time. But he did tell us where he got the gun. It seems Ritchie Stark threw it away, and Eddie decided to retrieve it from the dumpster. No use letting a perfectly good gun go to waste, which was a big break for us."

"Our Mr. Stark is stepping up in the world. He's done some shady things in his illustrous past, but mur-der hasn't been one."

At a stoplight Sam peered at her. "That we know of. We have several unsolved cases at the moment, the Sainsbury and O'Brien murders to name a couple."

"And your dad's attempted murder being at the top of the list."

"I've got a tip on where Stark is right now. I thought we would pick him up and have a little discussion with him down at the station."

Standing behind Sam, Becca studied Ritchie Stark as he sat at the table in an interview room, his dark hair slicked back, his beard cropped close. Thin to the point of almost looking like a scarecrow, he tapped his fingers against the wooden top, his eyes downcast.

"We've got you, Ritchie. You disposed of the weapon used to kill O'Brien." Sam leaned across the table, his eyes pinpoints.

"I found it! I ain't the violent type, so I thought I should throw it away. Didn't want no kid gettin' hold of it." Stark lifted his pointy chin, the tapping of his fingers increasing.

"Yeah, sure," Becca said with a humorless laugh. "Your fingerprint was found on one of the bullets still in the gun. Who hired you to kill Neil O'Brien?" She came around her partner to take the chair at the end, close to Stark.

"I ain't talking. I wanna see a lawyer."

"If you cooperate, I can convince the D.A. to go easy on you." Sam pushed to his feet. "If you don't—" he shrugged "—murdering a prominent city employee won't sit well with a judge or jury."

Tap. Tap. Tap. "I knows my rights. I wanna talk to my lawyer!"

Becca rose, too. "Sure, Ritchie. If you want to play

it out that way, life in prison with no parole is fitting for you. I personally don't think we should go easy on you." She started for the door, glad to get away from Stark's annoying drumming of his fingers on the table, a sure sign the man was lying. "You deserve to rot in prison."

While Sam stayed back, Becca left the room and watched through the two-way mirror at her partner and Stark, looking for any signs of the skinny man's armor cracking. Other than his nervous drumming, he remained tightlipped.

"I have pull with the D.A. I still can put in a good word if you cooperate. You aren't the one we want. We want the person behind everything," Sam said in parting.

Stark glared at the door that Sam had left through, his thin face pinched into a scowl.

"We'll let him stew for a while. Take our time getting him his lawyer." Sam moved to stand beside Becca.

"I know we cleared Colleen Montgomery of O'Brien's murder, but now there's no doubt she's innocent with this new proof." Becca thought of Quinn and his deep commitment to his family. She'd have to tell him the good news when she saw him next.

"Now all we have to find out is who was behind the murder and why?"

"Do you think there's a connection between Neil O'Brien, Baltasar Escalante and Dahlia Sainsbury?" Becca asked, her mind spinning with all the incidents that had occurred over the past few months in Colorado Springs, all wrapped up in the Vance and Montgomery families, who had been instrumental in Escalante's downfall the year before. But what kind of connection would there be between a fire chief and a drug lord?

After the incident in the tunnels below the museum the week before, she and Sam had learned from Alessandro Donato that Baltasar Escalante had been behind the drugs coming into the city recently, that he'd survived the plane crash last year and had a new face. When she thought of the drug lord, who was also a cold-blooded killer, being alive, she grew chilled. There was no love lost between him and the Montgomery and Vance families.

Again she pictured Quinn Montgomery with his russet hair, chocolate brown eyes and cocky smile that could melt a woman's heart. He could take care of himself, she was sure, but worry over his safety took hold and she couldn't shake off her concern. Someone had tried to burn his business down and had nearly succeeded, leaving only his offices intact. What if he had been in the shop or barn when it had been set on fire? The very thought sent another chill through her.

Standing before the full-length mirror on her bedroom door, Becca still couldn't believe she was wearing a sundress and sandals at home on her day off—her relaxing, lazy day. To make matters even worse she was wearing lipstick—this from a woman who didn't have time or patience to fool with putting on makeup. But Quinn would be here in a few minutes and for some insane reason she couldn't put on her usual attire of jean shorts, oversize T-shirt and no shoes. First capris and now a dress!

She heard a truck door slamming. Giving herself a once-over, she smoothed her hair, pleased that it was at least cooperating and turning under. Something else she usually didn't do was wear her hair down. What was the world coming to? Next she would be decked out in spiked heels, an evening gown and body glitter.

By the time Quinn rang the bell, Becca's hand was already on the handle. She opened the door for him. His smile of greeting did exactly what she was afraid of— sent a warm, fuzzy feeling zipping through her.

"Hi. You're right on time." Becca stepped to the side to allow Quinn into her house.

"I aim to please."

"That could be a company motto."

He turned to face her, his head tilted to the side, a thoughtful expression on his face. "You know, you're right. I may have to steal your idea."

"No, you don't. I gladly give it to you." She headed toward her living room. "Let's go in here."

As Becca sat on her beige and navy print couch, Quinn took the seat next to her. This was the largest room in her house and all of a sudden it felt as if it were the size of a closet. With her back straight, her hands folded in her lap, she tried to tamp down the racing of her heart. This was a business meeting, nothing else, and it certainly wasn't a date—she couldn't even believe she'd thought the word.

"Well, how bad is it?" Becca asked before the silence became uncomfortable and she started prattling.

"The estimate?" He opened his folder and took out a sheet of paper. "See for yourself. This will take care of the kitchen, the flooring in the attic and the ceiling in the bedroom."

Before she peered at the paper he held, she quipped, "Since your brother was a cop, you do realize how little we are paid?"

He chuckled. "Yes, you're definitely underpaid for the work you do. After what happened the other day, I'd double your pay."

Her gaze lifted to his. Suddenly they were back on the rooftop of the unfinished building, both trying to keep David James from jumping. A bond sparked the air, and Becca felt as if she had known Quinn well for years.

She broke their visual connection and reached for the paper. Her hand quivered as she grasped it and hoped he hadn't seen her reaction to what had just occurred. She didn't trust easily, having seen the seamy side of life for too many years. And yet there was something in Quinn that called to her, that urged her to put her trust in him.

After studying the figures, she said, "This is very reasonable. This includes replacing the cabinets in the kitchen?"

He nodded. "I'm going to do some of the work in the kitchen myself."

"You are? Why?" she asked without really thinking.

"Because I haven't had a chance to do a project like this in a long time and I'm treating myself. I miss working with my hands. Lately I've been doing too much of the administrative part of my job, especially with supervising the rebuilding of our barn and shop that was destroyed in the fire. So I've decided to personally oversee this renovation, if that's all right with you."

"All right? Yes, of course it is! I've heard Brendan talk about the staircase you carved in your house. It sounds exquisite."

"It took me four months, but I like how it turned out. I'll show you one day."

The thought of going to his house and seeing some of his work thrilled her. "I'd like that."

"Actually, if you've got some time today, I could take you now. I'm free for the rest of the afternoon."

"I'd be honored to see your work and—" she took the pen he held and signed the estimate "—I agree with your terms." Handing the paper back to him, she continued, "I never thought I would get personal attention from the owner of the company."

A dimple appeared in his cheek when he grinned. "The honor is all mine."

"When can you start?"

"Wednesday. I have a few things to clear up. We're moving our stuff back into the shop and barn tomorrow. It's been an intense couple of months getting everything done since the fire."

"I guess it pays to own a construction company."

"In this case, yes. I won't be taking security lightly, either. I've hired several extra people to look out for our offices and outlying buildings."

Relief flowed through her. "Good. I'm glad you're being careful."

"If you're a Vance or Montgomery lately in Colorado Springs, you have to be."

"Which reminds me, we arrested Ritchie Stark. He'll be charged in Neil O'Brien's murder." She started to stand.

"I know."

She halted in midmotion, slicing him a look. "How? It just happened late last night."

"Sam told me this morning at church."

Becca straightened, for a few seconds hovering over Quinn until he rose. He stood only a foot away, his clean, fresh scent that reminded her of a pine forest wafting to her. Dressed in tan slacks and a navy blue polo shirt, he looked like he had come right from church.

"What was Stark's motive?"

"He's not saying at the moment. He lawyered up. Maybe some jail time will loosen his tongue. I doubt he'll make bail."

"I keep wondering if all this is connected. Everything started with Max's attempted murder. I've been thinking—Escalante has to be behind the attempt on the mayor because of what happened last year. But what connection does Escalante have with Neil O'Brien? With Dahlia Sainsbury? Was Alessandro right about Dahlia working for Escalante? If so, why is she dead? What changed?"

Becca skirted her glass coffee table and snatched up her purse. "You ask some very good questions. Ones we hope to get answers to soon. Stark's arrest is our big break. Having suspicions is one thing. We need proof to hold up in a court of law." She withdrew her car keys. "I'll follow you to your house."

"I'll drive."

"But that means you have to come back here."

"I have to anyway. I need to get some measurements in your kitchen. I'll need a few things from my house."

"I have a yardstick."

"Not exactly what I need. It's only fifteen minutes away and remember, I have the whole afternoon."

"You sound like you don't know what to do with free time."

"Free time. What's that? I haven't had any in months."

"Then I insist you wait until Wednesday to start. I don't want to take away any of your free time. Believe me, I know how hard it is to come by."

"So we have established we're both workaholics," he said with a laugh, stepping outside onto the porch while she locked her front door.

"Is there any other way?"

"Actually, yes. Before Dad retired and I took over the business, I knew what a vacation meant. This is temporary for me. I don't intend for my whole life to be work. There's so much more to life."

Work was all she knew, Becca thought, not sure she could live any other way. "Vacation? What's that?"

"Perhaps I need to teach you how to play, Becca Hilliard."

The idea intrigued Becca more than she wanted to admit. Then she remembered all the unsolved cases of late and knew she wouldn't be playing anytime soon.

THREE

Quinn pulled into his driveway, wondering if the reason he was drawn to Becca was because they both needed to work less and play more. *God, are You trying to tell me something? I know I've been burning the candle at both ends lately. I plan to slow down—soon. I don't want to go back to how I was after Maggie's death. If You hadn't knocked some sense into me, I would have self-destructed.*

"Somehow I figured you for an ultramodern kind of guy." Becca gestured toward his large Victorian house, painted white with forest green shutters and a profusion of multicolored flowers adorning the beds along the front.

He switched off the engine. "Why?"

"I've seen a couple of the buildings your company has constructed. They're all glass and chrome."

"Not all the buildings. Besides, I have to follow the architect's plans. I execute someone else's dream."

She angled around so she faced him in the cab of his truck. "Did you want to be an architect?"

Her innocent question threw him back twelve years

in the past, to a time when he had been full of dreams. "At one time," he said, aware there was a pensive quality to his voice, but he couldn't disguise it.

"What happened?"

"Life's little unexpected twists. My father had a bad accident and needed me to run the business. He was laid up for almost a year. In fact, he still uses a cane because of that accident. I quit college and never went back even when he took over the reins again."

"Why not?"

He sucked in a deep breath and released it slowly. "I found I also love working with wood, making beautiful things. And my father needed me. The company was growing so fast and he couldn't do it all." Remembering the war that had raged inside him brought back a rush of emotions he hadn't experienced in years. He had wanted to return to college and finish his degree in architecture. His father had wanted him to continue working in the business so he could take it over one day.

"Family has a way of consuming our lives."

"Yes, but it's a good thing. I want a large one someday. You should see some of our family gatherings. Kids running all over the place. Laughter. Adamant discussions that never totally explode into an argument. That's why I went into the business. For the family."

Becca picked up her purse from the floor of the cab. "I know what you mean. After my mother passed away, it was either me raising my siblings or the state placing them in foster care. I couldn't let that happen. I quit college, got a secretarial job at the police station and took them in."

"When did you decide to become a police officer?"

"Almost from day one. But it was two years before I went to the police academy." A thin layer of perspiration coated her upper lip. With the air-conditioning off and the windows rolled up, heat began to build up in the small cab. "How about the grand tour?"

He laughed. "I'm not sure about the grand part, but I'll show you a few of the things I've done to my house. It might give you some ideas of possibilities for yours."

When Becca climbed from the truck, she scanned the lawn with its lush green grass, not a weed among the blades. Landscaped and well-tended beds added a richness to the front of the house with its orange, yellow and red flowers. "Do you like to do yard work, too?"

"Not my thing. I have someone come once a week to work in my yard. I love a beautiful lawn. I just don't want to do the work."

"A man after my own heart," Becca murmured, then realized what she had said. She didn't normally blurt out the first words that came into her mind, but with Quinn she found herself relaxing around him to the point where she had talked about things she usually kept private. Most unusual and not altogether unpleasant.

She mounted the stairs to the wraparound porch with forest green wicker furniture and a swing mounted from the ceiling. Her assessment of Quinn Montgomery was evolving and shifting the more she was around him. He was a wealthy, successful businessman, a prominent figure in Colorado Springs society, and yet he seemed so down-to-earth and nonchalant, except where it concerned his family, when a fierce protectiveness entered his demeanor. She liked that about the man.

When she stepped into his house, her breath caught at the beauty of the staircase that curved down from the second floor. Made of a rich mahogany, polished to a shine, its intricate carved railing made a sweeping statement of beauty as a person entered his house.

"You did this in four months? I'm impressed."

"I wanted something that would capture people's attention when they walked in."

"Well, you succeeded. How long have you lived here?"

"Almost four years. I bought this as a fixer-upper and just recently completed what I wanted to do with it."

Becca strolled into the living room off the large foyer, and again stood transfixed, taking in the beauty before her. The massive mahogany fireplace and mantel were every bit as intricate as the staircase. White crown molding accentuated the dark-taupe-painted walls and bookcases carved with swirls and leaves lined one wall. Glimpses at the titles of some of the books hinted at the man standing beside her. Historical books and biographies adorned the shelves, along with a few mysteries.

She walked closer to the bookcase. "Are you a history buff?"

"Yeah, you could say I am. I believe in order to understand the present you have to understand the past."

"I agree. People are shaped by their past."

"Exactly. Escalante has revenge in mind for the Vance and Montgomery families because of what happened last year. You can't escape your past, no matter how much you want to. It eventually catches up with you."

The tension in the warm, cozy room heightened. Becca didn't want to journey back any more into the past. She had given up her dream for her family and didn't regret raising her siblings. She would never have let them be raised by anyone else, but still she wondered from time to time what her life would have been like if the situation had been different. "How did we get on such a heavy topic?"

"Beats me."

His grin produced her own smile. "Show me your kitchen. I need some inspiration."

He swept his arm toward the dining room. A long table with clean, simple lines dominated the space. The maroon brocade on the eight chairs complemented the darkness of the cherrywood, adding an elegant tone to the room.

"You have excellent taste in furniture."

"Thank you. I just finished making that." He pointed toward a cabinet that housed a few pieces of a china set that looked old.

Its simple lines matched the table's, prompting Becca to ask, "Did you make everything in this room?"

"Everything in the house. I still have several rooms to finish."

"Do you ever sleep?" she asked, stunned by the amount of work that had to have gone into each piece of furniture.

"I don't require more than five or six hours, which

helps." He shrugged. "My brother says I don't have a life."

That was probably what many people would say about her. The connection she had felt that first day on the rooftop strengthened even more. "Is he right?"

His grin reappeared, self-mocking this time. "Yes. I'm working on changing that. I only work six days a week now. Sunday is my day off." He started toward a door on the other side of the room.

"But you're working today." Becca followed him into his kitchen.

His gaze snared hers and held it for a long moment. "This isn't work."

Her throat went dry and her pulse sped up. For several heartbeats she saw only him, before she tore her attention away and examined his kitchen, which was one of the reasons she was here.

"Wow," was all she could say as she swept her gaze around the room.

The first thing she felt was she would like to cook in his kitchen. This was a place where family would want to congregate, with its welcoming warmth in the dark tones of the cherry cabinets, its cream-colored marble countertops with various shades of brown swirls and its hardwood floor with a lustrous finish occasionally broken by an area rug that picked up the room's golden brown, dark red and forest green colors reflected in the plaid wallpaper. Her gaze rested upon what had to be the focal point, the built-in range with a mosaic tile pattern behind it on the wall with a glass-door cabinet flanking each side. Beautiful one-of-a-kind pieces of china and glassware were show-cased.

Quinn walked around, trailing his hand along the counter. "This is my mother's influence on my life. She felt the kitchen was the most important room in the house, therefore it should be put together first, which is what I did when I moved in here."

"I can see why you like to cook." A picture of herself creating some dish in this kitchen flashed into her thoughts and took hold. Its impact stole her breath. "You have carte blanche to do with my kitchen as you see fit. That is, anything within my meager budget."

The instant the words were out of her mouth she should have snatched them back. She didn't give control up easily and she had just given him free rein. From the wide-eyed look on his face her statement must have taken him just as much by surprise.

"What do you like in here?"

She spun around in a slow circle with her arms out-stretched. "Everything. But I suppose it wouldn't do for you to replicate your kitchen at my house, especially since this looks expensive."

"Not as much as you would think, but then I did the labor and I do have some resources." He paused, his gaze intent on her face. "You know you have to tell me more than that."

She lifted her shoulders. "I don't know. I just know I don't want what I have. It's cold, outdated and imprac-tical."

He sighed. "What's your favorite color?"

"Blue."

He started to say something else when she added, "But then I also like green, yellow and red."

His chuckles floated on the air. "Maybe it would be easier if I asked if there's a color you don't like."

"Hmm." She rubbed her finger along her chin and looked toward the ceiling. "Nope, not really."

"You're making this hard for me."

"But I like all colors. I don't really have one favorite. That should make it easier. You can't go wrong with any color scheme you pick."

"So you would be okay with purple and, say, orange?"

She winced. "Well, maybe not those two colors together, but I do like them combined with other colors."

With lightness deep in his eyes, he covered the short space between them. "Then I'll just have to get to know you better so I can figure out what will work best."

Words lodged in her throat, but for the life of her she couldn't voice any of them. Mesmerized by the deep chocolate of his eyes, she found herself being drawn into those rich depths, like a hot fudge sundae, lured from the safe, emotional world she had created for herself into an unknown one where feelings dominated and threatened to take over. And, like the sundae, both hot and cold, at the same time.

Swallowing several times, she blurted out, "I trust your judgment after seeing what you did with your house."

After she said that statement, surprise gripped her like a vise Quinn would work with. The day had been filled with one surprise after another. She took a step back to give herself some space because with him so near she obviously wasn't thinking straight at the moment. Trust wasn't something she often gave and especially when knowing someone for such a short time. What was it about Quinn that put her at ease? Yes, they had formed a bond up on the rooftop. Yes, she knew his younger brother, Brendan, and respected him. Yes, she had known who Quinn was casually. But those things weren't really what made her stay up at night thinking about him or doing something out of character like wearing a sundress, the only one she owned.

Puzzlement drew his eyebrows together. He combed his fingers through his hair before rubbing the back of his neck. "You've got to give me more than that. What do you like to cook? Fancy meals? Gourmet food? Simple fare?" A touch of desperation entered his eyes.

"Nothing fancy or gourmet, but I wouldn't classify it as simple, either. In the winter I love to make soups and stews. In the summer things like taco salad, three-bean salad. Then there's the old standbys like lasagna and spaghetti. I made things my sister and brother would eat. How's that help you?"

"I'm trying to get a feel for the work space you'd need."

"I don't cook as much anymore since Caitlin went into the Air Force a few months ago. With just me and my killer work schedule at times, it's hard to come home and fix a hot meal. But hopefully one day I'll do more."

Quinn leaned back against the counter and folded his arms across his chest. "No boyfriend to cook for?"

She glanced away from him. "I haven't had a lot of time to date much, especially now with working and going to school."

"What are you studying?"

"Psychology, with an emphasis on abnormal behavior. I took two classes during the spring semester, which practically did me in. This summer I'm taking it easy and only taking one, on Tuesday nights. I don't think it will be a hard class. I begin this week."

"Okay. This is a start. Let's go back to your house and let me get some measurements in the kitchen."

"For a man who doesn't work on Sunday, you're sure doing a good imitation of working."

"Measuring's nothing. I could do it in my sleep."

The mention of sleep brought Becca back to the fact that the past few nights—ever since Quinn and she had connected on the rooftop—she hadn't gotten a full night's rest. In her line of business that could be dangerous. She needed to exorcise the man from her thoughts, but then, that might be most difficult if he was in her house day after day renovating it.

"I thought all cops liked coffee and doughnuts," Quinn said, taking a seat at Becca's kitchen table later that afternoon.

She splayed her hand over her chest. "I'm crushed. You must watch too much TV."

"TV? What's that?" He couldn't remember the last time he had sat down to watch even the news.

"Occasionally I've caught glimpses of one in people's houses."

The twinkle in her eyes spoke to him on a level he hadn't responded to in a long time. Her renovation project was just what he needed to get back to what he loved doing at Montgomery Construction, what he had done before his father had retired. "I live on coffee," he said while Becca stood at the old stove waiting for a copper kettle to heat.

"I refuse to bring coffee into my house. Nasty stuff." Retrieving two mugs from the cabinet, she poured some hot water into each one and then dunked tea bags into them. "Here, try this. Tea is much better for you than coffee." After handing him a cup, she slid her own from the counter, then took the chair across from him. "This is chai tea. You can even have it cold if you like."

He stared at his mug as though it were a monster terrorizing him. "It looks like dirty dishwater." He sniffed it, a blend of spices peppering the air. "What in the world is in it? I like my coffee black, no sugar, strong."

She took a sip of hers, watching him over the rim of her mug, but she didn't say a word.

"If I try this, then you'll have to try my coffee. You haven't tasted coffee until you've had a cup of mine."

"You aren't gonna convert me."

Quinn smiled. "I've been told I have powers of persuasion."

Her laughter rang in the air, filling it with a sweet sound. "Sam's tried. Even your brother. Nope, I don't change my mind often once it's set."

He cupped the mug in his hands. "So no one can change your beliefs?" Somehow he got the impression they weren't talking about drinking tea or coffee but something much deeper. From a couple of comments she had said, he didn't think she believed in God. *Is that why You have nudged me toward Becca, Lord?*

"I'm slow to form an opinion but just as slow to let it go, too."

Quinn took a sip, winced, then firmly set the mug on the table. "Doesn't hold a candle to my coffee. Is that the best you have to offer?" He relaxed back in the chair, enjoying the lightheartedness of the conversation. So much had happened lately that was serious, it had been nice for a brief time this afternoon not to have to think about Escalante seeking revenge against his family.

She shot to her feet and stalked over to the cabinet, thrusting open its door. "Take your pick. I probably have thirty different kinds of tea for different moods."

"What mood is chai for?"

She narrowed her gaze, but that twinkle still danced in her depths. "It's for helping me to be patient." After closing the cabinet, she sat again and drank her tea as though she was seeking that patience she had talked about.

Sliding the mug away from himself, Quinn broke the silence with, "As I said before, I'd like to start Wednesday morning. I'll be in and out at first because I'm still overseeing a few projects. And since the explosion last month at the hospital, we will start rebuilding that physical-therapy wing soon. I'm training Chad Morrison to do some of what I've been doing."

"How do you want to handle getting into the house? I can have irregular hours and won't always be here in the morning to let you or your crew in. And I can't guarantee my neighbor will always be home, either. How do you suggest we do this?"

"You could give me a key."

Surprise danced across her face for a few seconds before she masked her expression and took a long sip of her hot tea. "That's probably the best way to handle it. It's just that…" Her voice faded into the silence.

"What? You don't trust anyone else with your key? Your neighbor has one."

"I've known Mrs. Williams all my life. She used to babysit me when I was young." She shifted in her chair and looked him right in the eye. "No, I'm not a very trusting person. I realize you'll have to have a key, but I would rather you be the only one who has access to it." She finished the last of her tea then added, "I know I don't have much to steal, but my personal space is very important to me."

"The renovation may be delayed at times. Are you okay with that?" he asked, her trust in him producing a grip on his heart that frightened him. There were too many similarities between Becca and Maggie, especially in their work. He was starting to care and that was just too risky.

She nodded, relief in her expression.

"Then we'll do it that way and anyone working here with me, of course, will be trustworthy. That's a promise."

His fervent look generated a tightness in her throat. She swallowed and said, "Great. I'll have one made. I'll make it a point to be here Wednesday to let you in and give it to you." She shook her head. "I should have thought about this before I decided to renovate. But as you can see, all I could think about was how much this house needs in order to come into the twenty-first century. Actually, I'm thinking the latter half of the twentieth century." She pointed toward the carved markings in several of the drawers. "That was done by my brother sixteen, maybe seventeen years ago. He got creative with a knife. Hey, maybe I should have pushed him in the direction of carpentry."

"I probably did some of that in my younger years. But what happened there?"

Becca glanced where Quinn was looking, even though she already knew what he was referring to. "That was the final straw. Last week the cabinet door fell off. That's when I decided I had to do something fast. Luckily I persuaded you to help me."

Closing the notepad he had been writing on, Quinn came to his feet. "I'd better be going. It's getting late and I have a meeting at church. I'm on the building committee. Go figure."

"No! I would say you are more than qualified."

He paused in collecting his elaborate tape measure, which put her yardstick to shame. "With God you don't have to have experience. He'll take you any way you want."

"If you say so," she murmured, remembering how the Lord had turned His back on her family. He took her father then her mother, leaving two small children without their parents and her as their only hope. Remembering that time submerged her in a renewed feeling of overwhelming helplessness she had fought hard not to experience ever again.

"I don't. The Bible does."

Her partner's faith was strong, and there had been a few times Sam had tried to talk to her about the Lord, but their partnership worked because he respected certain boundaries. She could remember crying and pleading with God to spare her mother. It hadn't helped. She'd still died, leaving her alone at twenty with two young siblings and no ready means of support.

Quinn headed for the front door. The quiet that had descended between them thickened. Before he left, he gave her a weak smile, a sadness in his eyes that made Becca feel she had let him down somehow.

As she closed and locked the door, she couldn't shake that feeling, and it bothered her that she cared what he thought. Her anger surged to the foreground. She marched back toward the kitchen to make herself another cup of tea, deciding it was best to keep Quinn at arm's length.

The blare of the phone startled her. Instead of going to the stove, she crossed the room and lifted the receiver. "Hello."

"Becca, this is Sam. I'm at the station. Stark is ready to cut a deal."

FOUR

"If you ask me, Ritchie—" Becca leaned close to the man who slouched at the table in the interview room, his clothes reeking of day old sweat "—claiming Dahlia is the one who hired you to kill O'Brien is mighty convenient since she's not around to defend herself."

Stark's thin shoulders hunched even more and a scowl creased deep lines into his brow. "I ain't lying. She's the one. Had me up to her big fancy office at the museum after hours so's no one would see us together. Never been in such a cold place."

Becca had felt the same way about Dahlia Sainsbury's office when she'd gone through it after the woman's murder. Maybe Stark was telling the truth. She lifted her gaze to Sam, who was lounging against the wall a few feet away. "There's no deal if we don't find evidence to support your accusations."

Sam sauntered forward, parking his body on the other side of Stark, who swiveled his head back and forth between him and Becca. "Got any suggestions where we can look for evidence to help your case?"

"Evidence? Like what?" The man rubbed his beard-covered chin, staring at the table before him.

"Let's start with why she would want Neil O'Brien killed." Becca straightened, his body odor churning her stomach.

Stark shrugged, his hands plopping down on the wooden top with a plunk. "I knew better than to ask why. I just followed orders."

"So you're just a lackey?" Sam backed off, too. "Working for a woman."

Stark glared at Sam. "She wasn't calling the shots. She took her orders from someone else."

Becca sat on the edge of the table, her arms folded over her chest. "Who?"

"Don't know. But she was followin' orders just like me. I knows these things."

"Did you ever hear her use the name Escalante?" Becca asked, hoping he was connected somehow to O'Brien's murder. It made sense that Escalante was with all that had happened the past few months.

"Es—Es—cal…" Stark shook his head. "All's I know is her."

Becca walked to the door and called an officer waiting outside the room to take Stark back to his cell. As he disappeared around the corner, Sam came to her side in the hallway.

"Looks like we have some more searching to do," she said, turning to her partner.

"We should start with her office at the museum tomorrow morning, since it's closed right now. I'll get the search warrants we'll need in the meantime. I don't want any lawyer able to exclude evidence if we're lucky enough to find some."

"Let's hope there's something there to help us, because we're running out of leads."

The sound of Becca's shoes on the blond hardwood flooring in the hallway of the Colorado Springs Impressionist Museum echoed as she and Sam approached Dahlia's office. The museum was nearly empty. The funeral for its curator was in a couple of hours. She and Sam would be attending.

Pushing open the door, Becca entered a few steps in front of Sam. She took in the various shades of cream, surprised there were so many of one color. The sparse furnishings and minimal personal touches left Becca with a cold feeling, as if Dahlia had meant to be in Colorado Springs only temporarily.

She headed for the desk situated before a large window that afforded a view of the front of the building and the street below. Perfect to keep an eye on who entered the museum, Becca thought as she pulled open the first drawer. While she carefully went through the desk, Sam checked a closet.

Backing out of it, he said, "Nothing. How about you? Anything of interest?"

"It doesn't look any different than when we went through it right after she was murdered. I was hoping with a different perspective there would be something that could help us." Becca shut the last drawer. "We need to check everywhere, even if it seems unlikely."

"Like the scene of a crime." Making his way to the

bookcase, Sam began to empty it, checking each item carefully as he did.

Becca rose from the cream-colored chair and ran her hands over its leather. She turned it over and looked in every crevice. She would take any scrap of information. After inspecting the desk chair, she strolled to the settee and examined it thoroughly. Tamping down her frustration, she moved on to the table and lamp next to the small couch.

"Maybe whoever murdered her took any evidence of her involvement, especially if that person was her cohort." Becca left the table and strode to the sand-colored brick wall, where an Impressionist painting hung. "I wonder if this is the real thing."

Sam glanced up from a book he was flipping through. "I'm no expert, but it looks like it is."

Becca read the signature on the oil canvas. "Monet. Wow. Even I know who he was. They let one of these just hang in here?"

Sam chuckled. "It is a museum with a good security system."

Becca hesitantly placed her hands on the sides of the painting, half expecting alarms to go off as she removed it from the wall. Carefully, she gently put it on the floor to examine it.

"You think she'd hide something in a Monet?"

Becca shrugged. "Just because she was an art lover doesn't mean she wouldn't use it if she thought it was to her advantage." Again she trailed her fingers over every square inch of the oil canvas and found nothing.

She hoisted it back up to rehang when she caught

sight of something funny looking. One brick appeared different, as though it had been removed then slipped back into the wall. The mortar around it was crumbling. Becca leaned the painting against the wall and stepped closer.

As she pried the brick out, she said, "Sam, I found something."

"What?" He covered the width of the office.

Becca stuck her hand into the hole, her fingers tingling. She'd seen a movie once where a person was tested by putting his hands into several containers, the contents hidden from view. In one was a deadly viper. She felt something cool to the touch. She probed the metal object. Quickly she withdrew her hand, clutching a key.

Sam stepped even closer and bent his head to inspect it in the palm of her hand. "Looks like a safety-deposit-box key."

"That would be my guess, but which bank?"

"Hopefully at a nearby one. We've got our work cut out for us, if not."

Becca closed her hand around the key and slipped it into her pocket. "Let's finish up. Maybe we'll find something else. Then we need to get to the funeral."

"It sure would solve some of our problems if Escalante decided to pay his last respects to Dahlia."

"But he's changed his appearance since the plane crash last year. Even with Alessandro's description it may be hard to tell who he is, especially if he's wearing a disguise."

"Yeah, I know." Sam walked across the office to complete his inspection of the massive bookcase along one brick wall. "Besides, if Dahlia was involved in the drug ring, that means she was a partner with Escalante. So did they have a falling out or did someone else kill her?"

"Even if they had a falling out, what would make Escalante kill her? She was still able to move freely around Colorado Springs, since we didn't have enough evidence to tie her to the drug ring."

"We need to delve deeper into Dahlia Sainsbury's background. Maybe we can find an answer to that question."

Becca moved on to the next picture on the wall, a pen-and-ink drawing of the Tower of London. It wasn't even noon and already the day was long. After the funeral she and Sam would go to Dahlia's apartment and search it again. She slid her hand into her pocket to reassure herself the key was there. Something told her this would be all they would find.

Becca cupped the mug of hot tea in her hands and breathed deeply of the orange and spices that flavored it. Scanning her kitchen, she noted another cabinet door hanging lopsided and was so glad that Quinn would start today. At least one thing in her life would get fixed.

After spending all day Tuesday calling banks in the area, she and Sam hadn't turned up where Dahlia's safety deposit box was until near closing time for the banks. She'd finally located one where Dahlia had opened a box recently. Sam would procure a search warrant first thing this morning, and they would drive to the bank outside Colorado Springs off the interstate going to Denver. Dahlia sure hadn't made it easy for them or for anyone else who might have discovered the key.

Becca blew out a long breath, then took a sip of her warm tea. Checking her watch, she realized Quinn should have arrived fifteen minutes ago. Hurriedly she finished eating her bran muffin and drinking her tea. As she took her plate and mug to the sink, the doorbell chimed.

Becca made a quick survey of her attire of black slacks, white short-sleeved shirt and comfortable black loafers. As she passed the mirror in the entry hall, she caught sight of herself and paused. The second she began to turn her head from side to side, she stopped, amazed at herself for worrying about her appearance. This wasn't like her at all!

Quinn would be coming to her home often over the next month, and she'd better get used to that and not fret about how she looked. Plastering a smile on her face, she swung the front door open. Quinn stood on her porch, appearing irresistibly handsome in faded jeans and a light-blue T-shirt with the name of his company on it. A thick brown leather tool belt encircled his waist. A cocky grin and a gleam deep in his brown eyes greeted her, sending her heart beating in double time.

"I hope I'm not too late," he said, his stance casual while Becca felt anything but casual.

The dimple that dented his cheek riveted her attention for a few long seconds before she managed to peer away and stare into those eyes that glinted with humor.

The beating of her heart kicked up another notch. Her mouth went dry.

Realizing she needed to say something, she cleared her throat and said, "C'mon in. I just finished breakfast. I have an extra muffin if you would like it."

He shook his head and came into her house, closing the door behind him. "I stopped by the Stagecoach Cafe, and Mom insisted I have a big breakfast. That's why I'm a little late. I should have known she would do that. One of these days I'll learn, especially if I have a place to be. She's just so sure I'm wasting away to nothing and every opportunity tries to stuff food down me."

Listening to him talk about his mother produced a memory from her childhood that she had tried not to recall. The morning her mother had received the news that her husband was being held hostage in a bank robbery burned itself into Becca's mind as though it had happened only yesterday. From that day forward she had been the strong one in the family. Her father had been one of the unlucky hostages and hadn't walked away from the bank. A gunman had shot her dad as a warning to the police not to mess with him. Her life, along with her whole family's, had changed forever after that. The memory produced a constriction in her throat.

Walking ahead of Quinn toward the kitchen, she was glad that he couldn't see her face. She was afraid of what he would discern. As a police office she'd learned to school her features into a bland expression—giving nothing away to a suspect that she didn't want them to know. As she entered the room, she kept her back to Quinn for a few extra seconds while she composed herself to present that neutral facade she'd become so good at.

Slowly she turned to face Quinn, whose attention was on the lopsided cabinet door. "Now you see why I need you." The instant she said that his gaze swung to hers, and she desperately wanted to retract what she had blurted out. "I mean, this kitchen is falling apart before my very eyes. I wouldn't be surprised if when you come next there'll be another door off. The hinges have to be from the turn of the twentieth century." She couldn't believe she was chattering like a nervous schoolgirl.

But she *was* nervous, she thought. There was something about Quinn that spoke to her and that scared her more than facing down a gunman. She licked her dry lips and went to her purse to retrieve his key so she could leave before she really said something she would regret.

"I aim to please," Quinn finally said, continuing his survey of the room. "I'm liking that motto more and more."

The humor in his voice eased her tension and she relaxed. Withdrawing the key from the bottom of her black leather purse, she covered the distance between them and held it out. His fingers brushed against hers as he took it. She was positive an electrical current had arced between them and run up her arm. Now she really was being ridiculous. That wasn't possible.

But his eyes widened for a few seconds as though

he felt the connection, too. He pulled his hand away and pocketed the key. "I'll be the only one to have this."

"Thanks. I appreciate you understanding about the key. You can never be too safe."

"Hey, my brother was a police officer, so I've gotten the lectures from him on several occasions, the last one being the fire at Montgomery Construction."

"You can take precautions, but if someone wants to get to you badly enough, they most likely will."

"But I'm not going to make it easy. Brendan and Ken Vance helped me beef up the security so hopefully nothing like that will happen again. But I won't breathe easy until Escalante is found. I'm sure he's behind everything that's been happening in Colorado Springs lately."

"Now that we know he's alive, we're searching for him."

"So are the FBI and DEA, since he's back to his old tricks again. But with his altered face it won't be easy. If he was behind the attempted murder of the mayor, which I'm sure he was, then that means he has been here for five months and we didn't know it until Alessandro encountered him in the caves under the museum."

Becca thought of Dahlia's safety deposit box. "Thinking Escalante is behind the murders is one thing. But we still have to prove it."

"Are you making any headway in that department?"

"We have a lead that Sam and I are following up on this morning." She glanced at her watch. "In fact, I'd better get going or my partner won't be too happy."

Quinn placed a tall red thermos on the counter by the

sink. "I hope it pans out because I don't like looking over my shoulder everywhere I go. Several times since the fire and bombing of the hospital wing, I've thought someone was watching me."

Becca paused in gathering up her purse and swung around to face him. "Why didn't you say something before now?"

He shrugged. "It's probably just my imagination."

"I've learned to listen to my inner voice. Don't discount your gut feeling."

"Oh, great, now I really am worried," he said with a chuckle.

She grinned. "Somehow I suspect you can take care of yourself," she said to alleviate his anxiety. He certainly was big and strong, but she would do the worrying for him. She'd talk to Sam and see if he knew of anyone else in the two families who felt he was being watched. "Lock the door after I leave," she tossed over her shoulder as she walked toward the back one.

When her hand was on the knob, he asked, "Will you tell me what became of the lead if I'm here when you get off today?"

She glanced over her shoulder, taking in his creased brow, his eyes that held concern. "Yes."

Later that morning at the bank, Becca waited until the door was closed, shutting her and Sam into the small windowless room near the safety-deposit-box vault, before she lifted the lid to peer inside the metal container. Seeing a black journal nestled within, she hurriedly removed it as though it would disappear if she didn't take possession of it. Sam crowded next to her, peeking over her shoulder as she opened the book and began to read.

"We've hit pay dirt," she said as she flipped through the pages, scanning the information laid out in the journal that Dahlia had written right after the incident in the tunnels with Escalante and Alessandro. "She names names." Becca tapped the page. "And here is the reason why I think Dahlia was killed. She's Alistair Barclay's half sister. I bet Escalante found out and didn't like the fact that his partner was related to the man I'm sure he had killed in prison for turning on him. That would explain quite a bit—one being why Dahlia kept a journal in the first place."

"Insurance in case something went wrong, which it did. She wanted Escalante to pay for her half brother's death." Flipping the page, Sam pointed to Harry Redding's name. "So he did shoot my uncle, which makes his apparent suicide even more suspicious. Another murder to add to the long list."

"And here's the information about O'Brien's murder, confirming it was Stark who had shot him. O'Brien wanted out. He thought he had repaid his gambling debts several times over with the hospital fire and arranging for someone to plant a bomb at the hospital. Obviously Escalante didn't and ordered him killed." Amazed at the information contained in the journal, Becca turned the next page and stopped, her gaze glued to a prominent name in the black book. "This is explosive. If it's true, and I can't see why it isn't, then this will definitely shake up Colorado Springs."

Sam frowned. "I shouldn't be surprised, but we need to do some checking before we bring in the deputy mayor for questioning."

"There should be a money trail somewhere that we can use to verify what Dahlia claims. We also need to have a handwriting expert confirm this is Dahlia's handwriting."

"Until then, let's keep this confidential."

"Yeah, your uncle doesn't need this on top of everything else that has happened to him since he was shot. Just think how easy it was for Dahlia and Escalante to operate with the acting mayor on their payroll."

Sam slammed the lid down on the safety deposit box. "As soon as we verify the money Dahlia claims she paid for Owen Frost to look the other way, we can have a little chat with the man and find out what he knows."

"If he'll talk." Becca hugged the journal against her chest, excited for the first real break in the myriad of cases they hadn't been able to solve over the past few months.

Becca parked her car next to her house and slipped from the front seat. Exhaustion leadened her steps toward her back door. She'd noticed Quinn's blue truck and looked forward to taking her mind off murders, suspects and money trails for a while. She'd been surprised he was still there since it was nearly eight o'clock, but glad he was.

The sun was slipping down below the mountains to the west as she pushed open her back door and entered her kitchen. She came to a halt. Before her the cabinets had been stripped from the walls. Earlier she had removed all the items to the dining room after her college class the night before, but seeing the sight made it clear she was finally doing something about her house.

Quinn glanced up from measuring a space by the refrigerator, a smile sliding across his mouth. "Long day?"

She nodded. For a flash, she imagined coming home after a tiring day to find Quinn waiting for her. The picture threw her off-kilter, and she nearly stumbled as she moved toward the table. Thankfully she was near enough to the chair to clasp its back and steady herself. "We have a lead we're tracking down."

"Can you tell me what?"

"Not yet. Soon. If it pans out, though, some questions may finally be answered." Actually, once everything in the journal was verified most of the questions would be answered—except where Escalante was hiding.

The radiance of his grin grew. "Good. It's about time." He put down his tape measure, peering at the kitchen clock. "I didn't realize it was so late. I'd better be going. I can imagine you're tired."

"Yes, but you don't have to rush off." She scanned the room. "You've certainly been busy today."

"I don't want you to be without a kitchen for too long. I'm gonna get this done first before we tackle the attic and ceiling in the bedroom."

She leaned into the chair, her grip on it tightening as a wave of exhaustion flowed through her. "I probably should have picked up something to eat on the way home. Didn't realize you would be so far along."

"I haven't eaten, either. Want to go with me to the Stagecoach Cafe and get some dinner? My treat."

Like a date? No, she decided, it was just Quinn being nice. The prospects of cooking didn't sit well with her. The prospects of being with Quinn did. She smiled and said, "That sounds great."

"Good. I hate eating alone."

"I know what you mean. Until recently my sister lived here, and it's been hard getting used to being by myself and cooking for just me."

"I'll give you pointers. I've got the cooking for one down pat." He unbuckled his tool belt. "I'll drive."

She didn't have the energy to argue that they should take separate cars so he didn't have to come back to her house and drop her off. After hours on the phone and looking at banking records, she and Sam had discovered the link between Owen Frost and Dahlia. Tomorrow they would bring him in for questioning. Until then she would enjoy her time with Quinn.

Twenty minutes later Becca climbed from Quinn's truck and walked next to him to the red barnlike nineteenth-century structure that housed the Stagecoach Cafe on South Cascade Avenue. Stepping inside was like stepping back in time, Becca thought as she scanned the rustic Western decor.

An older woman, attractive with vibrant red hair and twinkling brown eyes, hurried toward them. A smile creased lines into her well-preserved face, which resembled Quinn's. "Twice in one day. I must be living right, son."

A flush tinted Quinn's cheeks. "Mom, I see you all the time." When his mother's gaze slid to Becca, interest sparking in her brown depths, he added, "This is Becca Hilliard. Becca, this is Fiona Montgomery."

Becca offered her hand, which was ignored because Fiona embraced her instead, saying, "Nice to see you again. It's been a while since you and Brendan worked together. Quinn told me about the other day when poor David had his problem. Thankfully the D.A. won't be pressing charges against him, and I'm so glad he's getting the help he needs. No one should go through a crisis alone."

"I agree," Becca finally said, overwhelmed. Brendan had once told her that if anyone wanted to know what was going on in Colorado Springs, all they had to do was spend an hour with his mother. Now Becca understood what he meant.

"So why are you two here?"

"To eat," Quinn answered, looking around at the almost full café.

"Well, come this way. I think I can find a place for you two. It'll be in the back near the kitchen, however."

Becca didn't care if they sat in the kitchen. The aromas spicing the air—a blend of various meats, baking bread, cinnamon, onions and some smells she couldn't identify—knotted her stomach in hunger. She hadn't bothered with lunch except grabbing a bag of chips from the vending machine at the station.

As they threaded their way through the packed tables toward the back of the restaurant, Quinn said, "What are you doing here, Mom? You usually are gone by now."

Fiona threw her son a glance over her shoulder. "One

of my waitresses called in sick at the last minute so I'm filling in. When you own a business, you're at that business's mercy."

Becca took a seat at a red-checkered draped table with a small lantern in the middle that softly lit their surroundings, giving the place an almost romantic, intimate atmosphere, especially since the table was off to the side, away from the main body of diners. Fiona handed her a menu before rushing away.

Opening it, Becca peered over it at Quinn, who didn't bother to look at his. "Your mother is so full of energy."

"She's always amazed me. She's been here all day and is still going strong."

"I sure could use some of that energy right now."

"Tough day?"

Becca nodded then resumed her study of the dinner selections. She wouldn't be so tired if she weren't losing sleep over the man across from her. The night before she had tossed and turned for several hours. All she could think about was that Quinn would be spending time in her home over the next month—there sometimes more than she. His hands would be molding her kitchen into her dream room. The very idea caused her pulse to speed.

"Any recommendations?" she asked when she couldn't decide between several items.

"My favorite is the slow-roast buffalo fillet. Mom puts it on a bed of caramelized onions and peppers and smothers it with a boysenberry gravy."

Becca's mouth watered at his description. She slapped the menu closed. "Then that's what I'll have."

As if Fiona knew they had made up their minds, she reappeared with their waters, slices of lemon in them. She took their orders then hurried away.

Quinn watched his mother leave. "Most unusual."

"What?"

"She must be really busy. Usually when I come, she sits and fills me in on what's been happening."

"You just saw her this morning."

"That never stops her. She always has some news to impart."

"I've missed out on a source of information all these years," Becca said with a laugh.

"Believe it or not, Brendan has used her before."

"I don't eat out much unless it's to pick up something at a fast-food restaurant, but I'm thinking this may have to become a haunt of mine."

Quinn sipped his water. "I won't be able to work on your house until tomorrow afternoon. I have a meeting in the morning about the hospital wing."

"That's fine," Becca said, realizing that Quinn was a busy man. She was lucky to have him personally overseeing her renovations. With him supervising she didn't have to worry.

Fiona brought them their house salads. "Your dad will be delivering the apple pies for the barbecue early Saturday morning, so he can help you set up."

"Great. I sure appreciate you baking them for us. It'll be a treat."

Fiona turned toward Becca. "We're celebrating the

rebuilding of Montgomery Construction after the fire. Whoever did this can't get the Montgomerys down for long. I hope you'll join us."

Becca thought of all she needed to do and started to say no when Quinn added, "I hope so, too."

Becca shook her head. "I—"

"Son, I have to see to some customers. Talk her into it. Use that charm you have."

When the whirlwind known as Fiona left, Becca said, "I don't want to intrude on a family—"

Quinn held up his hand to stop her flow of words. "First, it isn't a family affair. It's a celebration for our family *and friends*. I definitely consider you a friend. I was going to ask you to come by before my mother jumped the gun. Before Saturday, if I know my mother, half of the city will be invited. I probably should order double the food I've planned."

"Still—"

He slipped his hand over hers on the table and her body responded as though the temperature in the café had soared ten degrees. "Please, Becca."

His gleaming eyes and dimpled cheek enticed her to let go of any reservations. His charm was in full force, she noted, relishing the warmth of his hand over hers. "Okay, if nothing comes up with the case." She really should have dated more. Then she would be better prepared for someone like Quinn, who was hard to say no to.

"I'll have to have a talk with Sam and make sure nothing does."

He removed his hand to pick up his fork to eat his

salad. Becca immediately missed the feel of his skin against hers. That thought sent panic through her. She hadn't really known Quinn for more than a week and already he was becoming important to her. Most unusual. She never plunged into anything. Caution was her middle name, right next to control and order.

Her gaze connected with his, the soft lighting casting his features in a warm glow. A sharp awareness of the man across from her trapped her breath in her throat. Suddenly, she felt as though all her caution was being thrown to the wind. Would control over her life and order follow?

FIVE

As the meeting with the mayor ended, Quinn stood and shook Maxwell Vance's hand. "It's always nice to do business with you. I promise you the New Hope Physical Therapy Wing will be completed again. I won't let some maniac get away with destroying something so vital. Montgomery Construction is dedicated to making sure it opens as quickly as possible. Next time the ribbon-cutting ceremony will take place. That's a promise." Quinn still remembered the last ribbon-cutting ceremony, which had been interrupted by a bomb blast that had left himself and others injured. Only recently had his ribs healed. Another incident he was sure Escalante was behind.

Max's hazel eyes, sharp and assessing, zeroed in on Quinn. His strong mouth clenched into a frown. "We both know Escalante is behind everything. Until he's caught, I pledge the necessary security to make it happen. To think of the destruction that bomb caused—and the injuries. It's hard to understand someone capable of that kind of evil—even someone like Escalante. But then I've seen so much in my sixty-eight years."

His world-weary tone made Quinn pause. "You sound like Dad. You ought to hear him rant about what Escalante has done."

"So much, though, that we can't prove, nor do we know where he is or what he really looks like. If he's changed his appearance once, what's stopping him from doing it again? He's gone insane with his revenge." The mayor released a deep sigh. "But hopefully Sam and his partner, Becca, will come up with where he is and catch him before someone else gets killed."

Quinn instantly pictured Becca in his mind and felt a smile slide across his mouth. Dinner at the Stagecoach Cafe had been interesting and fun, despite the fact that they both had been tired. "I'm sure they will. Both are good at their jobs."

"So you know Becca Hilliard? I didn't realize. But I was in a coma for quite some time."

"I'm renovating her kitchen."

"Renovating? I thought you were running Montgomery Construction now."

"I am, but I couldn't resist getting back to my roots and doing a hands-on project. I've missed that." *Plus, there's something about Becca that enticed me to accept her job personally.*

Max's eyes glinted with merriment. "Ah, and it doesn't hurt that Becca is an exceptional woman. Sam and she have known each other a long time. They even dated for a while. I thought at one time she would be my daughter-in-law."

For an instant jealousy roared to life in Quinn, taking him by surprise. He wasn't looking for a relationship with his crazy schedule and the threat hanging over his family. And besides, Sam was happily married to Jessica. No threat if he wanted—*stop right there,* Quinn admonished himself. *Remember? No relationships, especially with Escalante running around Colorado Springs, bent on destroying your family. And don't forget the line of work Becca is in.*

"Well, I won't keep you any longer. I'm sure, knowing Evie, she's shown up early for our appointment."

"Don't worry about the wing. Dad's coming out of retirement to take a personal interest in making it happen. When we get through, it'll be better than ever." Quinn started for the door with the mayor trailing behind him.

Stepping out into the reception area, Quinn came face-to-face with Yvette Duncan, fondly known as Evie. "It's good to see you again."

The strawberry blonde hugged him. "How's your mother doing? I haven't had a chance to go by the café in the past few weeks. I sure miss working with her."

"She could have used you last night. A waitress called in at the last minute, and she was running around trying to do several jobs at once."

Evie chuckled, her pale-blue eyes lighting up. "That sounds like Fiona."

"I'll tell her you said hi." Quinn moved toward the hallway, remembering the time that the councilwoman had hidden from her abusive husband and had worked at the Stagecoach Cafe. His mother's support had helped her get back on her feet.

Quinn started for the entrance when out of the

corner of his eye he saw Becca coming from the deputy mayor's office. He stopped to say hello. Behind her emerged Owen Frost and Sam. Quinn's gaze riveted to the deputy mayor's hands cuffed behind his back as Becca and Sam sandwiched the thin, red-haired man between them. Turning her head, Becca saw Quinn, the frown on her face replaced with a grin. She said something to Sam, then stopped in front of Quinn while Sam continued to escort Frost out of the building.

Quinn swung his attention back to Becca, so near him he could smell her light fragrance, which reminded him of something his mother baked. "This was the lead you couldn't say anything about last night?"

She nodded. "Owen Frost has been implicated in Escalante's ring."

Shocked at how far-reaching Escalante's tentacles were, Quinn struggled to keep his anger in check. "Do you think he had anything to do with Max's murder attempt?"

"Can't say right now. But believe me, Sam will find out. Right now we're looking into Neil O'Brien's murder and possibly Dahlia Sainsbury's. Even though Stark murdered O'Brien, we don't know how involved Frost was."

"I've never fully trusted the man, but involved in murder?" He peered at the door Frost had disappeared through. "What's his motive?"

"Most likely money." Becca hated not telling Quinn everything they had discovered in Dahlia's journal, that O'Brien's gambling debts had been the reason he'd set fire to the hospital wing and Montgomery Construction.

But she and Sam still had some details to check into before releasing the information.

"Now that wouldn't surprise me. He's always lived a little beyond his means."

"Hopefully we'll know more after we've had a talk with our deputy mayor."

"Does Max know?"

"Not yet. Sam'll call his father from the police station. He was in a meeting when we came by."

"With me."

"Ah, so that was the meeting you had."

"About the hospital wing. We're going to start rebuilding it now that the rubble has been cleared."

"Good. I didn't like going by the hospital and seeing the ruined wing."

"I'm meeting with Dad about it, then I'll be at your house for the afternoon."

Becca thought of the interview with Frost still to come and said, "I'd better go. This day will be another long one, especially if we manage to get any information from our deputy mayor."

"Good luck. I'd like this whole business settled soon so our lives can get back to normal."

"Normal. What's that?"

Becca started for the door, catching Quinn's smile. It sent a current of awareness through her as though when around him she knew every little detail involving him. It didn't take much to get a reaction out of her—a look, a touch, a smile. Boy, she needed to stay away from him. Quinn and Sam were so much alike, and it hadn't worked between Sam and her. Sam's faith—like

Quinn's—was important to him, whereas she'd given up on the Lord when He had taken both of her parents, leaving her to raise her siblings at the age of twenty, ill-equipped and unprepared to take on a ready-made family.

The minute she climbed into Sam's car he pulled out into the stream of traffic and headed for the station. She noticed her partner slide a glance toward her several times and knew he wanted details of what was going on between her and Quinn. Even though she and Sam had once dated, he was only a good friend now along with his wife, Jessica.

At the station Sam and she had to wait while Owen Frost was shown into an interview room where he met with his lawyer whom he had called from his office. They stood in the corridor, Sam's arms crossed over his chest while Becca wondered when her partner would bring up the subject of Quinn.

"Going to the barbecue Saturday?" he finally asked, unfolding his arms and straightening from the wall.

"Yes, and I'm going with Quinn."

"So you're dating him?"

"No. He's renovating my kitchen."

"But you're going to the barbecue with him?"

"He's just feeling sorry that my kitchen is a mess and giving me an opportunity to eat something other than fast food, which is about all I've had time for lately."

"Sure." Sam shook his head. "So that's what you've been telling yourself and everyone else."

Becca confronted Sam in the hallway. "Don't you read any more into it than there is."

Sam held up both hands. "You need a life outside work, Becca. Jessi and I are worried about you."

"Don't be. I'm too busy. I've started a new college course, and don't forget we have several unsolved murders that need solving."

"How can I forget when it involves my family—and Quinn's?" He leaned his shoulder against the wall, his relaxed pose back in place. "But still, Becca, you need more than work and school."

"Not everyone has to be married to be happy." She narrowed her gaze on him. "I've raised a family. Now I'm doing what I've wanted to do for years, finishing my degree."

"But there's more to marriage than having a family."

"Samuel Vance!"

"Okay, not another word from me…for the time being."

Frost's lawyer opened the door to the interview room, indicating they were through speaking. Becca moved forward, glad for the interruption. Sam could be very stubborn and downright nosy at times, which made him a great cop but exasperating as a friend who meant well.

Sam stood by the two-way mirror, his stance deceptively casual, while Becca took a seat across from Frost and his lawyer. On the surface her partner seemed relaxed, but she had worked with him long enough to feel the waves of tension emanating off him. They bounced off her own, making the atmosphere in the small room intense.

"We know you're taking bribes. We have proof that links you to Dahlia Sainsbury, Escalante and the drug ring. What do you know of the murders of Dahlia and Neil O'Brien and the attempted murder of Max Vance?"

Frost's thin face twisted into a frown. "I don't know where you got your info, but I'm not connected with either Escalante or Dahlia. I barely knew the woman. And I've never met anyone by the name of Escalante."

"Then those sums of money that appeared in your account on a regular basis had nothing to do with Dahlia paying you off to look the other way while drugs were being brought into Colorado Springs?"

"I haven't got the slightest idea what you're babbling about." The deputy mayor pinned her with a narrow look.

Sam rustled behind her and moved toward the table. He settled his fists on the wooden top, leaning his body halfway across the oak expanse. "If you know what's good for you, you'll come clean. People involved with Escalante don't have a long life. Perhaps you aren't familiar with what it's like in jail."

Frost drew himself up straight, his glare blasting first Sam then Becca. "I have nothing else to say to you."

"I'm putting an end to this interview," the lawyer interjected, standing. To his client, he added, "You won't be in here long. I'll make the arrangements."

"I'm not without some influence in this town. You'll regret this." Frost shot Becca, then Sam, another withering stare before leaving with his lawyer and a police officer to be processed.

Sam massaged the back of his neck. "I've got to call Dad and let him know what's going on. I'd hoped to have better news for him."

"We need to put a tail on Frost when he makes bail. Maybe he'll lead us to Escalante."

"Right now I can't come up with anything else better." Sam's shoulders slumped. "We've hit another dead end unless Frost talks, but that isn't looking too promising at the moment."

Rising, Becca put a hand on Sam's arm. "We'll unravel everything. We can keep digging into Frost's finances. And we'll delve deeper into Dahlia's past. See if Alistair Barclay was her only connection to Escalante before coming to Colorado Springs. Something else might come up."

"Yeah, maybe. I hope before someone else gets hurt."

Instantly the picture of Quinn popped into Becca's mind. She knew he could take care of himself, but what if something happened to him? The thought of not seeing his smiling face squeezed her stomach into a tight ball. Time was running out. Each day that passed without finding Escalante increased the chances of Quinn—or someone else—getting killed.

Dragging herself home that night, Becca let herself into the kitchen to find Quinn still working. This time she had bought some fast food on the way to her house, not expecting to see Quinn.

"You take your job seriously," she said, tossing the white sack onto her kitchen table, which was pushed to the side against one wall.

"I didn't get here until late. Besides, I wanted to know what Frost had to say."

"Nothing. He's out on bail as of an hour ago. We

didn't get anywhere." Becca tugged a chair out from the table and collapsed into it. "I don't have much, but you can share my fries."

Quinn snagged a seat next to her. "I was just about ready to give up on you. Talk about someone taking her job seriously. You've got me beat."

He was one of the reasons she was working so hard. His family, Sam's family, were in danger. She couldn't rest until Escalante and whoever else was working with him were brought in. But there was no way she would tell him that. "Yeah, a few people have accused me of being married to my job."

"You still coming on Saturday?"

"Wouldn't miss it. I hear it's gonna be the party of the month." And a great opportunity for Escalante to try something. If that was the case, she planned to be glued to Quinn's side. Then maybe she could prevent another tragedy.

He captured her gaze. "I realize it's a perfect time for him to strike. Believe me, I'm gonna have a lot of security, especially with the mayor being there."

Becca blinked, surprised at how easily he had read her mind. But the instant he had looked at her a connection, which had started on the rooftop, had sprung up between them, something she had never experienced before, even with Sam.

Quinn ran his finger down her jaw and tapped her chin. "You're tired. You're easy to read. And don't forget I know how a cop thinks. My brother was one."

She busied herself by taking out her hamburger and spreading her fries out on the ripped-open sack. She didn't like being easy to read. "Please. I don't really need all these. Help yourself." She took a bite of her sandwich.

"Well, maybe one or two, if you insist." He popped a fry into his mouth.

Becca scanned the kitchen, which, if it was possible, looked even messier than the night before. She liked order and this definitely was throwing her life out of order. She hadn't realized how much when she had come up with the plan to modernize her family home.

Quinn waved his hand toward the chaos. "The storm before the calm. By next week it'll begin to look like a kitchen again."

"Good. My life is crazy enough. Sometimes my timing is lousy."

"I don't know if there's ever a good time to tear your house apart."

"True," she said with a weak laugh.

Quinn took another fry. "You'll be glad when it's done."

Becca paused in bringing the burger to her mouth. "Just as you'll be when Escalante is finally caught once and for all."

"Yeah, it'll be nice not to feel like I'm walking around with a bull's eye on my back," Quinn said in a casual tone while sneaking another French fry.

"You're pretty calm about it. I don't know if I would be, and I'm a police officer."

"My life's in God's hands. I can't worry about the small stuff."

"Escalante after you isn't a *small* thing."

Munching on several more fries, he said, "That

doesn't mean I take unnecessary chances. But worrying about when you're going to die is wasted energy I don't have to waste."

Becca pushed the sack of fries toward Quinn. "Your faith means a lot to you."

"Of course. Without it, my life would have been like this kitchen, in total chaos. When Maggie died, I thought I had to. God dragged me out of my misery and showed me I still had some living to do."

"You don't blame Him for taking her away from you at such a young age?"

Quinn shook his head. "He didn't set the bomb. Maggie is in a better place now with God."

"But she had so much life ahead of her."

"Death is part of life. That won't change. What's important is how you live the life you're given, whether it is a few years or many."

That didn't stop her from wanting her father and mother to be alive. There was so much she wanted to share with them. There was so much they'd missed out on in their children's lives. *There was so much I missed because I had to take their place*. The thought came into Becca's mind unbidden but clear in its message. She'd been bitter about the role cast for her with her parents' deaths. Instead of making the best of it, she'd quietly fought it, never totally accepting it.

Chewing the last bite of her hamburger, Becca wondered what it would have been like if she'd had the kind of faith that Quinn had. Would she had been more settled in her life now? More accepting? Not as driven to capture what she had wanted all those years ago?

"You know, until my father's death we went to church every week." Becca wasn't sure why she had said that, but it felt right with Quinn.

"What happened?"

"Dad was killed in a hostage situation at a bank. My mother fell apart, which threw the family into turmoil. It was all I could do to get my sister and brother to school and take care of Mom. I think she died of a broken heart, even though the official diagnosis was cancer."

"I'm sorry." Quinn covered her hand resting on the table.

Its feel on hers comforted her as the memories of long ago tumbled through her mind, bringing forth the pain she had kept locked inside while dealing with her mother's illness and raising her siblings. A lump clogged her throat, surprising Becca since she hadn't cried in years.

"Dad had been very involved in church. I was one of the leaders of the youth group." For a long time she had repressed those memories—of the fun times she'd had at church with her friends. It had been easy to blame God for all that had happened.

"Did your minister try to help you after your father's death?"

"Yes, but I wouldn't listen to him. The man who had killed my dad was dead in the shootout. There wasn't anyone to lash out at...."

"Except God."

Becca nodded, staring down at his hand still over hers. The link brought her solace as she journeyed into the past with fresh eyes. What would have happened to her if she had turned to God, not away?

"Come with me to church on Sunday."

Becca tugged her hand free. "I don't know. I have—"

"Please, Becca. Give God a chance again. Let Him heal your pain."

"I'm not hurting anymore," she said too quickly.

Quinn arched an eyebrow. "You aren't? Are you so sure of that? Have you really let go of the anger over your parents' deaths?"

"Have you let go of your anger over Maggie's?" Becca suddenly wanted to lash out at him, wound him as he had her with his questions.

His intense look drilled into her. "Anger, yes. Sorrow, no. There'll always be a small part of me that will mourn her loss. I loved her. She was going to be my wife."

Becca held his gaze for a long moment, then peered away, the pressure in her chest growing with emotions she didn't take out and examine often. "I'm sorry. I didn't mean to say that."

"Yes, you did. You wanted me to hurt as you are. The difference, Becca, is that I've given my pain over to the Lord. Will you come to church on Sunday with me?"

She drew in a deep, composing breath, relieving some of the tightness in her chest. "Okay, but I'm not guaranteeing anything."

"Just open your heart and mind and listen. That's all I ask."

Weariness weighed heavy on her shoulders. She sagged against the chair's back. She needed to lighten the mood. "What will people say? First the barbecue and then church together, all in the same weekend. They may begin to think of us as a couple."

Quinn tossed back his head and laughed. "I know what my mother will think. All her matchmaking skills will come to the foreground. So beware."

"I like your mother."

"Well, she won't rest until each of her children is married, which only leaves me. She wants a whole passel of grandchildren. The only reason you escaped the third degree the other night was because she was filling in for that ill waitress. Otherwise she would have been parked at our table."

"So I'd better hide from her Saturday?" Becca could see Quinn as a father.

"If you know what's good for you."

This time Becca laughed, enjoying the moment after such a long day of trying to find answers and not succeeding. "You know I thrive on a challenge."

"Then you and I have something in common. I thrive on one, too."

His direct look that delved beneath her defenses left her without a reply. Somehow she was sure he was referring to something else beside his mother. Did he think he could reconcile her with the Lord? The thought didn't bother her as much as it would have a month ago. Maybe he was right. Maybe she needed to let go of the past and the pain, turn it over to the Lord as he had.

Quinn finished off the last fry, a smile splitting his face. "I guess I was hungry after all. Sorry you didn't get any."

"I didn't need them. Got to watch the weight. When

I'm on a difficult case, I tend to eat more than I should, as if food will take care of the problems. And the foods I eat are all the wrong kind."

His gaze trekked down her, leaving a warm trail where it touched. She swallowed hard and snatched up the sack, crushing it into a ball. Rising on shaky legs, she hurried to the trash can in the corner, needing to put some space between them. Suddenly the room was way too hot, as though the air-conditioning had stopped working.

"I guess I'd better get going. I'll be here tomorrow morning early. I'll only be able to work half a day, though. I still have a few things to do before the barbecue."

Relief, mixed with regret, trembled through Becca. He wouldn't be here tomorrow evening when she came home. Two nights in a row was more than she could handle at the moment. Quinn Montgomery was lethal to her peace of mind. She needed to get a handle on the feelings he generated in her or he would distract her from the cases she needed to concentrate fully on.

He strode toward the back door. Becca followed, intending to lock it after him. Instead, she went outside on the back stoop to watch him leave. She loved how he walked, so self-assured, not a wasted movement. But he didn't step off the porch. He turned toward her, the small space between them shrinking to half a foot.

His nearness produced a fluttering in the region of her heart. The light from the kitchen shadowed the hard planes of his face. But she sensed his penetrating gaze on her. Her mouth felt as if she had trudged through the desert for days without water.

He inched closer, invading her personal space. "I'll pick you up on Saturday at ten."

"You don't have to. I can drive myself there. I'm sure you'll have a million things to do right before."

"If I'm not ready by then, a half an hour won't make any difference. Besides my mother will be making sure everything is in its right place. I'll let Brendan and Dad be at her beck and call."

"Ah, I see."

"You don't know Mom. She can be a tyrant right before a party."

"Then I'll be ready at ten."

She didn't think it was possible for him to get any closer, but he did. When she brushed against him, her pulse kicked into a rapid speed, causing each breath she took to be shallow. Tilting up her chin, he looked into her eyes. She couldn't read his gaze, but she didn't have to. His intentions vibrated the air between them. He was going to kiss her.

Slowly he bent toward her, whispering his lips across hers, sending tingles down her spine. She shivered from the sensations bombarding her. Again his mouth teased hers, not really settling on hers. A gentle touch. A total possession even though he never really kissed her. When he pulled back, she wanted so much more, but the danger in that was great. She could lose her heart to Quinn, whose faith was strong, who would make a wonderful family man. She would never fit into his life.

Before she found herself lost in his embrace, she backed away, pressing herself against her screen door as far away from Quinn as possible on the small stoop. "I'll see you Saturday." Was that her voice that quavered with each word uttered? She felt the heat of a blush flood her cheeks. She never blushed, and yet Quinn had managed to cause one.

As he strode toward his truck, her fingertips grazed across her lips and she thought: *What else would he manage to change in her life?*

Quinn pulled into the parking space next to the renovated barn that now housed the offices of Montgomery Construction. Switching off the engine, he twisted toward Becca, taking in her turquoise-and-hot-pink sundress. He doubted he had been very successful in hiding his surprise when he had seen her at her house. Most of the time she dressed in tailored navy or black pantsuits. She looked dynamite in a dress that emphasized her small waist and long legs, her feet clad in hot pink sandals.

"The fire gave me an excuse to change things around. I'm utilizing the barn more. It has such character that I couldn't resist," he finally said, dragging his gaze away from her toes, which were painted hot pink. He just had never thought of Becca Hilliard as a hot pink kind of gal. This side of her intrigued him. What else would he discover?

"You can't miss it," she said with a laugh, her attention on the bright fire-engine-red structure before her.

He shrugged. "It seemed appropriate." He waved his hand toward a more sedate building to the left. "That's the new warehouse. The old one was completely destroyed in the fire."

"What's that?" Becca pointed toward a smaller building to the right of the barn.

"Our workshop."

"Where you create your masterpieces?"

"Sometimes when I have time I work here, but usually I use my workshop at home."

A red Mustang pulled up next to Quinn's truck as a SUV came into the parking lot. "Everyone's starting to arrive." After climbing from his vehicle, Quinn began to round the front of it, but Becca was out before he had a chance.

She offered him a grin. "Sorry. Used to opening my own doors."

"It's good to see you here, Becca." Brendan, with Chloe and her two children, came up to them. "My brother has finally gotten smart."

Quinn groaned. "I expect it from Mom, but not you."

"Before those two forget that we're even here, it's good to see you again under nicer circumstances, Becca. These are my children, Kyle and Madison." Chloe stuck her hand out toward Becca.

She took it and shook it. "Brendan has mentioned your kids on more than one occasion."

"Mom, can we go get something to drink?" Kyle asked, hanging back from the group with his sister next to him.

"Sure, but only one soda." After her two kids hurried around the side of the barn toward the big tent set up in back, Chloe said, "I hope you can catch who's been behind all that's happened lately in Colorado Springs. I heard about Dahlia's murder and Owen Frost's arrest.

I can still remember my own run-in with the man who tried to kill the mayor." She shivered, hugging herself.

Brendan slipped an arm around Chloe. "You're safe."

She looked up at him. "I don't think anyone is safe until Escalante is caught."

"I agree with Chloe," Quinn said, the hairs on the nape of his neck tingling as though someone were watching them.

He scanned the terrain surrounding Montgomery Construction. Anyone could be hiding in the trees that edged his property on the north and east sides. Although a tall electrified fence, turned off for the day, enclosed the company site, he felt vulnerable, even with added security. He realized when he had built back everything that was destroyed that he had made it bigger and better as if he was taunting Escalante to try and demolish what he had created. But Quinn itched to face the cold-blooded killer and make him pay for what he had done to his family. No one hurt his family and expected to walk away unscathed.

SIX

With binoculars, Escalante stood in the shadow of the forest next to Montgomery Construction and watched Quinn Montgomery talking to his brother. Escalante knew the instant Quinn sensed his presence. The man surveyed the perimeter, his hands balling at his sides.

Escalante cackled. Quinn's time would come, as that of others in his family. "I've destroyed this once. I can again." Pleasure at the thought of watching the red barn go up in red flames brought a wide smile to his face.

As his mind started making plans, Escalante caught sight of a couple with a small boy approaching Quinn. Dark-complexioned with black hair, the toddler hid his face against Peter Vance's neck.

Escalante's anger skyrocketed. *Manuel. His son. In his enemy's arms.*

The strong urge to charge into the compound and grab his only living child overwhelmed Escalante, his vision blurring with his rage. His hands gripping the binoculars tightened until pain forced him to release his hold. The binoculars thudded to the forest floor.

Sucking in deep breaths, Escalante managed to calm himself enough to realize this wasn't the time. But he wouldn't wait long. Manuel belonged with him. He was an Escalante, not a Vance, no matter what a piece of paper said.

They will all perish and I will take back what is mine.

"I don't know how you do it," Becca said, holding one of Jessica and Sam's twins.

Jessica cradled Dario to her, gently rocking him back and forth to get him to sleep. "Having two at once is definitely a challenge, but it's all worth it. Besides, Amy adores her little brother and sister and helps whenever she can."

"As Sam does. I'm constantly getting updates on each stage they're going through."

Jessica situated Dario in his stroller to sleep, then took Isabella from Becca to place her next to her brother. "That's my husband. He wants another one soon."

"Glad it's you, not me."

Straightening, Jessica looked at Becca. "You'd make a wonderful mother. You're so good with Dario and Isabella."

"Been there, done that," she said, but the words didn't come as easily to her lips as previously. It did feel good to hold Isabella in her arms, to have the baby nestle against her chest, grabbing whatever she could. The baby scent still lingered in the air, producing memories of the times she had helped her mother with her younger sister and brother. She had enjoyed her role of big sis, just like Amy.

"Where did Sam and Quinn go?"

Becca scanned the large tent, the aromas of hamburgers, hot dogs and barbecue chicken spicing the air. "I don't know. Quinn said something about showing Sam the plans for the new wing for Vance Memorial."

Julianna Red Feather approached Becca and Jessica. "I was so glad to see the last piece of rubble removed the other day." A shudder shook her body. "Too many memories associated with it."

Ken Vance came up behind Julianna and took her hand, kissing it. "Thankfully you and Angel came to my rescue."

Becca recalled the chaos after the bomb explosion that had destroyed the hospital wing. Julianna and her search-and-rescue dog, Angel, had been instrumental in rescuing more than Ken. Quinn had narrowly escaped, too. How many times would it take before Escalante succeeded in finally hurting him? The thought sent her own shudder down her length.

"Ah, here come Sam and Quinn with Amy trailing along," Jessica announced, pushing her stroller out of the way so her twins could take a nap.

Becca's heartbeat increased as she spied Quinn weaving his way through his guests, his gaze on her. For a long moment the people around her faded from her consciousness, and she could only see Quinn, a grin on his face, his eyes lit with appreciation. Her heartbeat kicked up another notch. She had to tear her gaze from his before she hyperventilated.

"Have you seen the plans for the new wing?" Sam

asked Ken as they joined them. "Granddad would be proud to have his name over the hospital entrance."

"Yeah, Julianna showed me the other day when I picked her up from work." He sent his date a look that spoke volumes. "Even better than it was before the explosion."

Becca wondered when those two would announce their engagement. Ever since Ken had come to work for Quinn and been thrown together with Julianna, they had grown close. In fact, Becca surveyed the crowd around her and realized that many were couples now. A pang pierced her. Suddenly she felt like a little girl staring into a toy store's window at a ten-speed bike, but too poor to buy it. Being on the outside looking in had never bothered her before. She'd always been so busy she'd never had time to worry about it. But now that her sister and brother were raised she had the time—no, she didn't. She wanted to finish her degree, which had gotten interrupted ten years ago when her mother had died. She wanted to fix up her house, something that had been needed for years. But mostly she wanted to solve these murders before— She wouldn't go there. Quinn was safe. She would make sure of that.

A cry erupted from the stroller. Before Jessica or Sam could move to it, Quinn lifted Dario up, cooing to him and making silly faces at him. The baby settled down, studying the man holding him. Becca watched as Quinn cuddled Dario and gently rocked him, quieting the child, whose eyes fluttered close. Before long, Quinn had Dario asleep again and back in the stroller, reinforcing Becca's observation that he would make a wonderful father and should have many children.

"You're good, Montgomery. Where'd you learn that?" Ken asked.

Quinn gestured about him, Amy and Madison running past them, giggling. "Do I have to say more? There are almost more children here than adults. I think the Vance and Montgomery families are trying to see who can have the most babies."

Holly Vance Montgomery arrived in time to hear Quinn's statement. "I belong to both families now and have done my part." She patted her rounded stomach. "Well, almost. Hopefully soon."

Jake Montgomery joined his wife, handing her a tall glass of iced tea. "You can say that again. This waiting is killing me."

"I'd be a basket case. I'm not very good at waiting," Quinn said, his look slipping to Becca.

She had to concentrate to keep her cheeks from flushing. For a few crazy seconds she could picture herself pregnant with his child, waiting for the birth. The vision scared her. "I think I'll see if your mother needs any help," she murmured and escaped the group of happy couples, feeling at a disadvantage with her and Quinn the only two not dating—well, not dating seriously.

Becca headed toward the table where the food was being put out. "Can I help?"

Fiona glanced up from putting down a bowl of potato salad and smiled. That was when Becca realized her mistake. She'd gone from the frying pan into the fire.

"Why, sure, hon. I still have a few more dishes to bring out from the kitchen in the barn."

Becca hurried away, thinking she had escaped an interrogation by a pro, when she found Quinn's mother keeping pace with her. "I can get the items for you."

"Nonsense. With both of us bringing the food out, it'll be on the table twice as fast. I have a feeling we have a mob of hungry people waiting for me to serve them." She laughed. "But I'm used to that because of the café."

Becca opened the side door into the barn and came to a halt. She hadn't come into the building yet and was stunned by its transformation. "Barn" was no longer a word she would apply to the structure. Yes, there was a big open space in the middle with offices opening onto it on the two floors. The building still retained a feel of a barn with its rustic decor and Western theme, but that was where the resemblance stopped. Everything else was modern and reeked of an office complex of a multimillion-dollar business.

"It still surprises me," Fiona said near her ear. "Quinn had been wanting to redo the offices for some time. Told his dad he wanted to bring the company into the twenty-first century. So I guess some good came out of the fire that nearly destroyed everything. Escalante didn't count on that. The kitchen is this way." Fiona preceded Becca across the large central area where several groupings of tan leather couches and chairs were arranged with large Navajo rugs adding a colorful richness to the decor.

As Quinn's mom opened the refrigerator door and began removing bowls, she asked, "How long have you known my son?"

The woman's tone was casual but behind the words there was a sharp interest in the answer. "I've known who he is for several years, but until last week we hadn't seen each other much. As you know, I responded to the suicide at his construction site."

"Didn't you used to work in missing persons?"

"Last year. Not long after helping Sam with finding Jessica's little girl, I transferred to homicide and have been teaming up with Sam as his partner."

"You're in a dangerous profession. Quinn was engaged to a police officer a few years back."

Becca could see the wheels turning in Fiona's mind as she tried to gauge how serious she and Quinn were and how her job would affect their relationship. "I didn't know Maggie well, but she was a fine officer." She paused, deciding whether to set the record straight or not. The concern in Fiona's expression prompted Becca to add, "Quinn and I are just friends. He's helping me with renovating my house, which sorely needs it. That's all." If Becca said it enough, she would begin to believe that was all they were, that the past few days meant nothing to either one of them, that they hadn't shared a bond since that morning on the roof of the unfinished building.

Fiona shot her another look full of questions. "Most unusual. Quinn hasn't gone out with many women since Maggie's death. So seeing you two together twice in a few days made me wonder if there was something going on. He was in a bad way for a long time. Like all mothers, it's hard for me not to worry about my children."

Becca filled her hands and arms with as many dishes

as she could manage. "I didn't get to tell you the other night how much I enjoyed the meal at your café." Knowing when she was being interrogated, she needed to change the subject. She certainly understood Quinn's mother's interest because she would be that way if her brother or sister were seeing someone.

"Do you all need any help?" Quinn asked from the doorway into the kitchen.

Becca whirled around and almost dropped one of the bowls she had cradled against her chest. "I didn't hear you come in." How much had he heard?

Quinn hurried across the room and removed two dishes from her hands. "We've got a hungry crowd out there. I thought I'd see what was taking so long." His penetrating gaze bore into hers.

He'd heard at least part of the conversation, Becca decided, if his look was any indication.

His mouth quirked up in a grin. He leaned close to her ear as he turned toward the door and whispered, "I thought you needed rescuing." He sauntered toward the entrance.

Becca watched him for a few seconds, her body reacting to his nearness in a traitorous, uncharacteristic way—sweaty palms, rapid pulse, heated cheeks. She wasn't used to this happening to her!

Fiona started forward. "Better not keep them waiting any longer then."

Fiona's movement snapped Becca out of her daze. She gripped the bowls tighter, hoping she didn't drop them, and followed the pair out of the barn into the bright June sunlight.

* * *

Becca sat at a table under the tent, the late-afternoon sun hot, only a light breeze cooling the day off. Most of the guests had left, with only a few still at the barbecue.

"I think this party was a success," Quinn said, seated next to her.

"It was so successful, especially the games for the children, that you've tuckered out my son." Emily held Manuel in her lap, his eyelids drooping, then popping open only to shut again.

"As usual he's fighting sleep. He doesn't want to miss any action." Peter stood and took his son from his wife. "We'd better leave and get him home."

Sam approached the table. "Leaving?"

"Yeah. Manuel loves sleeping in the car. If Emily and I are lucky, he'll remain asleep when we get home and we can get some things done around the house."

Emily gathered up her diaper bag and purse. "Thanks for inviting us, Quinn. I'm so glad everything is back on track for you."

Sam took the chair that Emily had vacated on the other side of Becca. "I'm glad nothing happened today. I get jumpy when a large group of Vances or Montgomerys get together."

Quinn frowned. "We can't live our lives in fear of Escalante. If we do, he's won."

"Just the same, I'll feel better when I catch him. Did either of you feel like we were being watched?"

Becca nodded at the same time as Quinn did. "I think he's got us all jumpy."

"I had enough security here that if he had he would have been caught. Escalante isn't a stupid man. I wasn't gonna let anything interfere with this celebration." Steel edged Quinn's voice as determination lined his face. Rising, he continued, "I need to check with Mom and Dad about the cleanup crew, then I'll take you home, Becca."

The worry in Sam's expression caused Becca to ask, "What's eating you?"

"Now that we know for sure Escalante is alive, I need to tell you something that could be a problem. Peter and Emily's child, Manuel, is Escalante's son. He doesn't know about Manuel, at least I hope not, but if we don't find the man soon, he could discover he has a son alive. It's not common knowledge. Only the immediate family knows. We didn't say anything even when we thought Escalante was dead. Manuel doesn't need that."

Becca shifted, facing her partner. "What's Peter doing about it?"

"He's keeping a close eye on his son. He thought about leaving Colorado Springs until Escalante is caught and he may still. But he didn't want to raise suspicion by leaving suddenly. He may, though, after Colleen's wedding in a few weeks."

"Peter does have the know-how to protect his son. But we'll just have to find Escalante. That way he won't have to keep Manuel in a prison."

Sam grinned. "That's my thinking. We need to put some pressure on Frost."

"We can make the case against him so strong that his only option is to make a deal."

"But that will take time."

And time was their enemy, Becca thought.

"Ready to go?" Quinn asked as he came up to the table.

Becca stood, placing a hand on Sam's shoulder. "First thing Monday we'll start with each person we know who was working for Escalante. There's got to be a clue to his whereabouts."

On the walk around to the front of the barn where Quinn's truck was parked, he said, "You could cut the tension with a knife today at the party. Toward the end I think people were relaxing some, but I could tell each one was wondering what would happen next and to whom."

"Makes you wonder if creating tense anticipation isn't part of Escalante's plan."

"Well, if it is, it's working." Quinn reached around Becca and opened her door.

"We'll get him," Becca said when Quinn climbed in behind the steering wheel.

He tossed her a grin. "I'm so glad you two are on the case."

His compliment warmed Becca's insides. She prided herself on doing a good job and now more than ever it was important that she solve these murders and catch Escalante. Quinn's life could be in jeopardy if she didn't. The thought of anything happening to him was unthinkable.

When he pulled into her driveway, Quinn escorted her up to her front door. Although the sun was going down behind the mountains, Becca didn't want the day to end just yet.

"Want to come in? I have some lemonade and iced tea and I can still get to the refrigerator to get it."

"Sure. I'll take a glass of iced tea. I had enough lemonade to float a boat today."

As Becca led the way into her house, she thought of her denial to Quinn's mother that they were dating, and yet it felt as though they had been on a date. She'd even invited him in after going out.

Determined to put a business reason to her invitation, Becca brought him a tall glass of iced tea into the living room and asked, "Do you think the hole in the bedroom ceiling will be fixed by the Fourth of July weekend? My sister will be home for a few days."

After she sat on the couch, Quinn eased down next to her. "I can do it any time you want. Let me get the kitchen a little further along and I'll do it next."

My, the room seems awfully small suddenly—and warm. She resisted the urge to fan herself and instead drank deeply of her iced tea, relishing its refreshing peach taste as it went down. "I always knew there were a lot of Vances and Montgomerys, but I didn't realize how many until I saw so many in one location."

"Wait until tomorrow. We take up quite a bit of the pews at the Good Shepherd Christian Church." Quinn took a long sip of his drink.

Church with his whole clan. She didn't get intimidated by too much, but the thought sent a bolt of panic through her. "I doubt you ever get lonely with so much family here in Colorado Springs."

"Not for long. Do you miss your brother and sister?"

"The house is certainly quiet. Neither lives too far

away, but yes, there are times I wish the house was full of people." She gestured around her. "This is a big house. Too big for just one, but it's been in the family a long time, so I don't see myself downsizing."

Quinn relaxed against the back cushion, running his arm along it and angling toward her. "I know what you mean. I bought my house with the idea of starting a family with Maggie. When she was killed, I seriously thought of selling the place. But it became one of the things that kept me sane. I threw myself into fixing it up. Some days I worked so long all I could do was fall into bed still dressed, but exhausted. I didn't even have the energy to get changed. I didn't have the time to dwell on my loss, either."

"You can't run from a loss forever." He was so near she could lay her hand over his heart and feel it beat beneath her palm. She wanted to, as if that would take his pain away from his loss, but instead she laced her fingers together in her lap.

"I've dealt with Maggie's death."

"Your mom said something about you not having dated much since Maggie died. She wanted to know if we were dating. She definitely wants those grandchildren."

Quinn groaned. "Sorry about that. I knew she was gonna quiz you about us when I saw her heading into the kitchen with you. I tried to get in there but Dad stopped me."

"You should have a house full of children. You were great with the kids today." The memory of him refereeing the games only emphasized that in her mind.

"And as I told my mother, one day I will. I want a large family." He grinned, a dimple appearing in his cheek. "After all, I have a large house that needs to be filled."

"A full house?"

"At least three, maybe four."

Three? Four? Becca gulped, her throat suddenly parched. If she had thought there might be more between her and Quinn, that pretty much took care of that notion. If she ever married, the most children she would want was one, and only after several years without any.

"How about you?" Quinn asked and downed the last of his tea.

He would have to ask. But then it was probably best to make her position clear. "Maybe one when I'm older." Until recently she hadn't even thought she would have one child. What had changed? "Of course, I need to have that husband first." She laughed, a shaky one at best, not sure she liked what was happening to her. If she stayed around Quinn too much longer, she would declare she wanted to have a whole basketball team of kids, then be faced with having to raise them.

"You're so good with Sam's twins. You handled Isabella's crying like a pro. Some single people run for the hills when a baby does that."

"Jessica was busy feeding Dario, and Sam was nowhere to be found. Besides, I helped raised my brother and sister from when they were babies. I was quite a bit older and loved to help my parents even before they died."

His eyes gleamed, focused totally on her. "I could tell you had a lot of experience."

The air in the room seemed to be sucked away. She drew in a breath but couldn't get a decent one. Her lungs burned from the probing of his gaze as though he sought to know the inner her. Very few people knew the real Becca because she didn't trust easily. Yet with Quinn she found herself telling him things she didn't talk about with others, especially someone she hadn't known for long.

"You could say that. I was basically my siblings' mother from twelve on, ever since my sister was born. Mom was…fragile. Dad did what he could but he worked a lot. Then when my father died, my mother fell apart and couldn't handle much. She got sicker and depended on me even more."

"So you didn't have much of a childhood?"

"Don't get me wrong. I love my brother and sister and wouldn't have changed my time with them for anything, but no, I didn't do all the things my friends did. I didn't go on my senior class trip. I didn't date. I didn't have time for extracurricular activities at school."

Quinn cupped her cheek, bending toward her, his gaze locked on hers. "So it's your time now?"

"I think it's a little late for me to go to my prom, to go out for cheerleader or to join a club."

"No, I meant date."

The air completely left her lungs or so it seemed. Words flew from her mind. Suddenly all she could think about was his hand gliding through her hair and gently urging her toward his lips.

Vaguely she thought: *Too dangerous. Pull away before you lose your heart to him!*

She didn't, couldn't. His mouth settled over hers, and she felt as if she had come home. He wrapped his arms around her, drawing her even closer until she was sure he could feel her heart hammering against her rib cage. As he deepened the kiss, all the reasons a relationship with Quinn wouldn't work in the long run fled her mind. All she could zero in on was the touch of his lips on hers, the warmth and comfort of his embrace.

When he finally pulled back, resting his forehead against hers, his ragged breathing mirrored hers. In that moment she knew he had been as affected as she by their first real kiss. That revelation was heady—and frightening.

"I'd better leave," he said into the silence that had descended between them as they both tried to gather their composure.

"Yes," she murmured, wanting his mouth caressing hers again and feeling bereft it wasn't. "I had a great time today. The food was wonderful, but then your mother was in charge of it, so of course it was. But having fun can be tiring." She was babbling, she thought, aghast at herself. She didn't babble! She didn't fuss over how she looked, either. Quinn Montgomery was throwing her life into chaos in more ways than just in her kitchen.

He unfolded his long length and stood. "I'll pick you up at ten tomorrow morning."

"Yes, ten," she murmured, already trying to decide what to wear. It had been years since she had gone to church.

Quinn took her hand and led her toward her front

door. "It's casual attire," he said as though he could read her mind.

She swallowed the gasp his words produced, amazed at his ability to be so attuned to her.

When he stepped out onto the porch, Becca followed. Night had settled over the landscape while Quinn was visiting. The street lamp illuminated his truck in her drive for all the world to see. It looked so right parked there.

He started down the steps, stopped and turned back to her. Tugging her against him, he planted a quick kiss on her mouth, then proceeded toward his truck, leaving her stunned by its powerful effect.

When he reached his pickup and opened its door, the interior light lit the area up. That was when she saw his back tire.

"Quinn, you've got a flat."

He jerked around. "What?"

"Your back tire is flat."

He left his door open and investigated while Becca walked to him. When he straightened, he said, "Someone slashed it."

He went around his truck, checking each tire. Becca ran her hand over the rubber and felt the knife gash.

"All of them have been slashed. This one even has the knife still in it."

"Don't touch it."

"Sorry. I already did."

Becca hurried around to the other side where Quinn was. "That's okay. Leave it. There may be fingerprints on it."

"I don't need fingerprints to know who did this."

"Escalante," Becca said, making a slow circle as if she could see into the dark shadows that suddenly seemed sinister.

SEVEN

Quinn moved forward in the line at the back of the church by the door. "Pastor Gabriel, this is Becca Hilliard. She's Sam's partner."

Becca took the minister's hand. "I enjoyed your sermon."

"Thank you." Reverend Gabriel Dawson looked deep into her eyes. "I hope you visit us again."

Placing his hand at the small of her back, Quinn guided her toward the door, saying, "I'll see what I can do about that."

Out in the foyer Becca started for the church's entrance, trying to make sense of her conflicting emotions that had come to the foreground ever since Pastor Gabriel gave his sermon. He could have been personally talking to her.

"Let all bitterness, and wrath, and anger, and clamor, and evil speaking, be put away from you, with all malice. And be ye kind one to another, tenderhearted, forgiving one another, even as God for Christ's sake hath forgiven you."

Is that why I stopped going to church? I was angry at You for taking my parents? For robbing me of what I had planned to do with my life? The questions tumbled through her mind, producing more. *Was I so wrapped up in the negative that I couldn't see the positive in my situation?*

"Becca." Quinn lay his hand on her shoulder. "There's refreshments in the rec hall."

She blinked, so focused on her thoughts that for a few seconds Quinn's words didn't register.

"Becca, are you all right? Do you want to leave?"

She shook her head. "Sorry. I was thinking about the sermon."

His mouth, which only the night before had kissed hers, tilted upward. "Don't be sorry about that. Pastor Gabriel gives thought-provoking sermons. I'm glad you see that."

He led her toward the rec hall where a table of cookies, coffee and punch was set up. The children crowded around the refreshments while the adults stayed back, talking in small groups.

"Hey, cousin. Recovered from your big shindig yesterday?" Colleen Montgomery sidestepped to give Quinn and Becca room in the circle.

"Working on it. Really should be asking Mom and Dad that. They shouldered most of the work. When did you get into town?"

"We arrived late last night. Otherwise, we'd have been at your barbecue."

"I hear you will be starting on rebuilding the hospital

wing," Alessandro, Colleen's fiancé, said. "With all your other projects, that will be a lot of extra time."

"That's why Dad's coming back to Montgomery Construction. He wants to head up the rebuilding of the wing."

"I think Uncle Joe is tired of retirement."

"You might be right, Colleen." Quinn shifted closer to Becca as Sam approached. "Especially with Mom at the café all the time."

"You only have a few more weeks until the big day. I don't know how you can put a wedding together so quickly," Becca said, noticing Sam's frown.

"Between my mom and Aunt Fiona I'm not having to do much."

"Becca, we need to go."

The urgency in Sam's voice riveted her attention as well as everyone else's. "What's wrong?" *Please not another murder, God.*

"Someone just tried to kill Frost."

Colleen perked up. "Is he hurt?"

"No. I would prefer you not do anything with this information at the moment."

"I'm not working as a reporter anymore so your info is safe with me." Colleen winked at her fiancé. "I've had a better offer from Alessandro."

While Sam started for the entrance, Becca twisted toward Quinn. "Thanks for bringing me. I'll talk to you later."

Concern etched his features. "Call me when you get home."

Becca heard Colleen quiz Quinn about their relationship as Becca hurried after Sam, who waited for her in the foyer. Quinn stated to his cousin that she was just a good friend. Hearing him say what she had been saying about their relationship sent disappointment through her. Seeing yet another happy couple caused dreams to dance in her mind.

You can't have it both ways, Hilliard, she told herself as she fell into step beside Sam.

"I'm glad to see you at church today," Sam said as he switched on his car.

She didn't want him to start in about her attendance with Quinn, not when she was feeling such confusion. Instead she asked, "Did Frost ask to see us?"

"Yes, he's at his house with his lawyer and some police officers."

"I think Escalante is the one responsible for slashing Quinn's tires last night at my house. So it seems he has been extra busy lately. Maybe this will be to our advantage for a change."

Sam threw her a surprised look. "I hadn't heard about Quinn's tires. Escalante's getting bold and reckless. That means he'll make a mistake soon."

"I hope before he kills again."

Becca couldn't get the picture of Quinn out of her mind as he had dealt with the situation. Determination had clenched his jaw and hands. Silence had pulsated in the air as she'd waited with him for the auto-club tow truck to come and remove his truck. Quinn had refused to go inside, as though he were taunting Escalante to make an appearance. She'd kept guard, with her weapon near, worried that Escalante was out there in the dark watching and waiting to finish Quinn off. By the time the tow truck had arrived, tension had blanketed them both in sweat. That had been the longest thirty minutes of her life.

"Quinn got the message," Becca said, staring out her side window. "Escalante wants us to know he can get to anyone, anytime."

"That might work in our favor with Frost." Sam pulled up in front of the deputy mayor's house, parking behind two squad cars.

Becca nodded at the two police officers standing guard on the porch. "Frost inside?"

"Yes, ma'am. He's in the living room waiting for you two."

Becca went into the foyer, and waited for Sam. She whispered to her partner, "In there." She nodded toward where Frost was. "Ask me about how I felt having Escalante slash Quinn's tires in my driveway."

Sam grinned, a gleam sparking his eyes as he did exactly that.

Becca started for the living room. "Escalante has nothing to lose, that's for sure. Vandalizing a truck in a police officer's driveway proves that. No one is safe until we get him." She kept her voice pitched low but not too low that Frost didn't hear every word.

"And you were right inside the house when he did it and didn't hear a thing." Sam stepped into the entrance and immediately said, "We'll talk more later."

Frost's normally ruddy face was ashen, as though he had been sick for several weeks. His demeanor contained none of the cocky assurance of a few days ago.

He sat with his lawyer on his cream-colored couch, twisting his hands together. Becca immediately thought of Dahlia's office and its cream-colored decor.

"I hope you aren't wasting our time, Mr. Frost. I'm in no mood for it today." Becca marched into the room, dark with all the drapes closed, and positioned herself in front of the deputy mayor as though she was ready for a battle—which she was. Quinn's life was at risk, and she wasn't going to let Frost stand in the way of catching Escalante.

Sam came to her side and murmured, "I understand why you're upset, and believe me, you have every right to be, but let's hear what our deputy mayor has to say first."

Becca wanted to applaud Sam's performance of good cop/bad cop. They often traded off being the tough or sympathetic one. Right now she relished the role of the tough cop. It gave her a way to vent some of her frustration over the unsolved cases. "Okay, Mr. Frost, why have you called us here? Didn't the officers take your information on this alleged attempt on your life?"

"Alleged attempt!" Frost shot to his feet, stomped over to the drawn drapes and shoved them back. He pointed toward the large window that afforded him a view of the front of his house. "Just in case you don't know what that is, it's a bullet hole. If I hadn't bent over to pick up a magazine from my coffee table, I'd be dead. Dead!" The dark brocade drape fell back into place, throwing the room into dimness except for the lone lamp on by the couch.

Becca followed the path the bullet would have

probably traveled and found it lodged in the mantel about four or five feet off the floor. "We'll get the crime-scene unit out here. That's about all we can do besides canvas the neighbors to see if anyone saw anything." She started toward the entrance. "We'll file a report, though I don't see why the first officers on scene couldn't have done this."

"That's all you're going to do?" Frost's voice shrilled the question. "I am the deputy mayor of Colorado Springs! I deserve—"

"Not for long," Becca cut into his tirade, having already heard rumors that Max wanted Evie Duncan, someone he could trust, to take over that position until he was fully recovered.

"As my partner said, there isn't much else we can do," Sam said in a level voice. "It was probably Escalante, but unless we find him, there isn't much we can do about the threat. I hate to tell you, but we have to have evidence to go on before we can make a move."

"Probably wasn't even Escalante. I bet Mr. Frost did this himself to get sympathy." Becca shifted toward the entrance again.

"I know where Escalante might be," Frost said, his cheeks singed with red splotches. "The man's crazy. Dahlia said that several times. I didn't have anything to do with any murders. I was paid to look the other way when the drugs started coming into the town, that's all."

That's all! Becca bit down on her lower lip to keep her opinion inside. The man was talking and she didn't want to stop him.

"I'll tell you what I know from my meetings with Dahlia. I tried to find out anything I could in case I needed the information later. But I'm not saying a word until I am promised around-the-clock police protection until Escalante is caught."

"You've got it." Becca moved back to Sam's side.

"I want a deal from the D.A. for immunity from all charges."

"That may take some time, and I don't know if he'll do that. The charges against you are serious ones." Becca again clenched her teeth to keep from saying something she would regret later. She hated the fact that they sometimes had to make deals with criminals to catch bigger criminals.

"My lawyer will go with you and work out the deal with the D.A. I'd like to stay here with protection until it's worked out."

Sam scanned the living room with all the drapes closed, the only barrier between Frost and the outside. "Wouldn't you be better down at the police station until they can hash out the details?"

"No way. Look what happened to Alistair Barclay. He was murdered in jail. I feel safer here for the time being."

"Even after what happened this morning?" Becca heard the contempt in her voice and tried to curb it. They were so close to a good lead on Escalante's whereabouts.

"Yes." Frost settled back on the couch, trying to appear nonchalant but not succeeding with his balled hands and stiff posture.

Frost's lawyer gathered up his briefcase and said to Becca, "I'll meet you at the D.A.'s office."

"It's Sunday," Sam said.

"I suggest you get ahold of him and get him down to his office to make a deal. Unless you're not serious about wanting to catch Escalante."

Becca nodded toward Sam. "We'll meet you there."

Out in his car a few minutes later, Sam watched the lawyer climb into his vehicle. "Next time I get to play bad cop. It took all my willpower not to go after Frost and demand he tell me where Escalante is."

Becca studied her partner, whose hands grasped the steering wheel so tightly his knuckles were white. "Will you be able to do this? I realize with your father—"

"Don't go there, Becca. I've been on this case too long not to be there at the end. So yes, I will be able to do whatever it takes."

"Even let Frost walk for the information he gives us?"

The rigid set to Sam's jaw attested to his anger, barely held in check. "Yes, if it gets us Escalante. So the info better be worth it."

Becca silently thought the same thing. Sam had his family to worry about. She had Quinn.

Night cloaked her house in darkness as Becca pulled into her driveway late that day. Quinn's blue truck parked next to her house brought a frown to her face. He wasn't supposed to be working. Was something wrong? The evening before came crashing back down on her, and anger burned through her at the thought of Escalante sneaking up to Quinn's truck, slashing the tires. In her driveway! With her only yards away!

She quickly slid from her car, scanning the terrain, half expecting to see Escalante in the shadows. This had to end. Her nerves were so taut she was afraid they would snap at the least little thing.

She headed up the driveway. After hours of negotiation between the D.A. and Frost's lawyer, they had come to an agreement. Frost would spend minimal time in prison for his part in the drug ring and Escalante's schemes. From his information, she and Sam had discovered that Dahlia had purchased some land almost five months ago near Cripple Creek. Frost didn't know the exact location, but he did know that Dahlia didn't like anything having to do with the outdoors or rugged country. Why would she purchase land she never intended to use? That was a good question and one they would pursue first thing tomorrow morning.

"Becca."

A deep male voice came to her from her front porch. She stopped by his truck and stared into the darkness. "Quinn? What are you doing here?"

"I was waiting for you to come home."

"How long?"

"Not long. I called the station and talked to Sam. He said you two had just finished interviewing Frost and you were on your way home."

Becca mounted the steps to the porch. "Is something wrong?"

"I wanted to make sure everything was okay. You've been working so hard lately, putting in extra time on your day off. I was worried about you."

She wasn't used to people being worried about her.

The gesture brought a lump to her throat. Boy, she must be tired if she was getting emotional over something like that. "I'm fine. When I'm on a case, I can get driven. The longer the case goes unsolved the harder it is to solve."

"Hence the long, long hours?" Quinn rose from the wicker love seat and covered the distance between them.

"Part of the job."

He touched her arm. "Have you eaten tonight?"

She nodded then realized he probably couldn't see the movement in the dark and said, "Yeah, Sam and I grabbed something before our interview with Frost this evening."

"Did you find out anything useful?"

"Maybe. I'll let you know if it pans out."

He moved even closer until Becca could smell his distinctive aftershave. "You know I have a vested interest in seeing Escalante brought in. Maybe I could help."

"No," she said too quickly, a vision of Quinn getting shot by Escalante flashing across her mind. "It's legwork that Sam and I can handle." There was no way she would tell him that she wanted to protect him from Escalante. He probably wouldn't appreciate the gesture. Besides, she couldn't involve a civilian in police work.

His hand skimmed up the length of her arm until he cupped her face and brought her within inches of him. "We'll have to do dinner some other night."

His mouth was a breath away from hers. She nodded again, his nearness robbing her of the ability to speak.

"I can't work on your kitchen tomorrow, but I'll be here bright and early Tuesday."

She inhaled a shallow breath that didn't meet her need for oxygen. All her senses were centered on the feel of his warm, rough palm against her cheek. His hand burned into her skin, making a mockery of her declaration they were just friends. There was definitely more to their relationship than being friends—had been from the very beginning.

He slid his lips across hers. She shivered and he drew her closer. His mouth explored hers, then left a trail of tiny kisses to her ear. Clinging to him, she savored the moment of bliss she experienced in his embrace.

When he parted, his hands framed her face, and she felt the intense exploration of his regard, even though darkness surrounded them. "You know, we can't keep telling everyone we are just friends."

"What are we?" she managed to get out, backing away so she could breathe.

"Dating."

"Probably not a good idea."

"Probably not."

"The timing is all off."

"If you say so. But Escalante won't be out there for long. I have faith that you and Sam will catch him."

"That doesn't change the fact that we don't agree on several important issues. You want a family. I don't. Your faith is strong. Mine is shaky at best."

He put several feet between them, leaning back against the railing. "I know. Not to mention I'm not fond of your profession."

"Then why are we wasting each other's time?"

"Good question." Raking his hand through his hair, he shrugged. "I can't help myself. Feelings aren't always logical."

"The wise course of action would be not to see each other."

"Not practical. I'm doing your house."

"You could turn it over to someone else," she said, not really wanting him to.

"No." He straightened. "When I start a job, I finish it. I'll see you Tuesday."

When Becca watched him walk to his truck, she saw a shadowy movement in the dark. While he pulled out of her driveway, she scanned the area, wondering where Escalante was. Maybe her life would become more normal once he was caught. Maybe she could sort through this labyrinth of emotions, all centered around Quinn Montgomery.

"I haven't seen your mom tonight," Becca said, taking a bite of her house salad with a raspberry vinaigrette dressing.

Quinn chuckled. "Because I did some snooping and discovered that she isn't working tonight. After the barbecue Saturday, I figured you needed a break. Where do you think Brendan got his interrogation techniques from?"

"She means well. She only has your best interests in mind." Becca relaxed back in the chair now that she knew that Quinn's mother wouldn't pop out of the Stagecoach Cafe's kitchen to ask what her intentions were toward her son.

"That's why I tolerate it. Mom's the best, but she wants to know everything going on in her children's lives, as well as everyone else's."

"Having been a surrogate mother with my siblings, I understand where she's coming from."

"Is your sister the only one coming home over the Fourth?"

"Yes. My brother can't get away."

"Then I'll have to meet him some other time."

The statement implied a relationship beyond the renovation, and Becca responded with, "Are you sure you're up to that? He takes his job as the man of the family quite seriously."

"When it comes to family, I'm an expert. With such a large one, no one is capable of minding their own business."

"I owe you a dinner. This is the second one you've treated me to. But you'll have to wait until a certain carpenter finishes with my kitchen."

"I have a kitchen you can use at any time."

"How about this Saturday night I treat you to one of my home-cooked meals?"

"You've got yourself a date."

There was that word again. She might as well admit that they were dating, as Quinn had suggested. She couldn't continue fooling herself into thinking they were just friends. It was more than that—much more.

"And speaking of a date, I need one for Colleen's rehearsal dinner next Friday and for her wedding on Saturday. Care to come with me?" He wiggled his eyebrows and quirked a grin.

"You've got yourself a date." Becca finished the last of her salad, her hunger pangs partially satisfied. She knew better than to skip lunch, since she hadn't had much for breakfast, but all her and Sam's work had finally paid off. "I have some good news."

Quinn perked up, his gaze swinging to hers. "About Escalante?"

"Yes. Sam and I think we've narrowed down his location to three places near Cripple Creek."

"Where Michael Vance lives?"

"One isn't too far from Michael's ranch, so that's the one we are concentrating on. We can't get a warrant because we don't have probable cause, so we're staking out each place to see who comes and goes." Becca had never shared an investigation with an outsider before, but she couldn't contain her excitement and she trusted Quinn. That spoke volumes about the depth of her feelings toward him. She liked coming home, like tonight, and finding him at her house. It felt so right that it scared her.

He lifted his water glass. "Here's to getting the man soon so we can get back to our normal lives."

She clinked her tea against his drink. "I'm all for that. Normal is good."

Quinn's gaze narrowed on something beyond her. "Looks like normal won't happen tonight. Mom's making a beeline for us."

Becca glanced over her shoulder and saw Fiona negotiating her way toward the table, stopping to say a few words to several of the customers on her trek toward them. The woman's indifferent expression didn't fool Becca.

"The food here is great, but I've got to find another restaurant," Quinn muttered as his mother came to a halt by their table.

"Hello, Becca. It's good to see you again. I hope the food is to your liking. Quinn, you should have told me that you were coming to eat here tonight. I'd have made sure we had your favorite dessert. We're all out of pecan pie."

"Pecan pie? Not apple pie?" Becca asked, suppressing a laugh that bubbled up.

Before Quinn could answer, Fiona said, "Oh, no. Every birthday instead of a cake, he's always insisted on a pecan pie."

"I'll survive without a piece of pie tonight." He blushed. "Is another waitress ill?"

"No, I like to come by sometimes and make sure everything is running smoothly."

"Sure. 'Fess up, Mom. You're here because someone called to tell you I was here eating with Becca."

Fiona waved her hand in the air. "Well, that, too. My staff knows I like to be kept informed of what's going on here."

Quinn threw back his head and laughed. "The staff knows you are a busybody."

"Quinn Montgomery, I am not a busybody."

"Mom?"

Her mouth twisted into a pout. "Okay, maybe a little. But I only want to make sure the people I care about are happy."

Becca was enjoying the exchange between Quinn and his mother. A warmth infused the banter that proclaimed the strong, comfortable relationship they had.

"Would you like to join—" Her cell vibrated at her waist, cutting off her invitation. "Excuse me," Becca said to the pair and flipped open her phone, tension gripping her as she noted who was calling. "Hilliard here."

"We have a woman who has barricaded herself and her family in her house on Taylor Street."

"I'm on my way." She bolted to her feet as she clipped her cell at her waist. "I have a hostage situation."

Quinn rose, tossing down his napkin. "I'll take you."

"Thanks." Becca knew that time could be an enemy or a friend in a barricaded situation. She needed to get there as quickly as possible to assess which it would be.

Becca started for the entrance while Quinn said to his mother, "Talk to you later."

"Go. I hope everything works out. I'll be praying, son."

"Thanks."

Quinn caught up with Becca as she left the café. Her professional demeanor had fallen into place as they emerged from the restaurant. Having seen her in action, he knew she was a capable negotiator who took her job very seriously. Much like Maggie had been as a bomb expert. But one bomb had become her enemy and taken her life.

As he headed toward the address Becca gave him, fear planted itself in him, and there was nothing he could do to keep it tamped down. Anything could happen in a hostage situation, and Becca would be right in the middle of it all.

EIGHT

The chill of the air that swept down from the mountains encased Quinn as he stood behind the perimeter barrier to the house on Taylor Street, lit with spotlights that had been brought in to see what was going on. Becca sat in the command center, but several yards away, talking on the phone to a woman threatening suicide.

He should have gone home hours ago but couldn't drag himself away. Becca had been negotiating with the woman for the past seven hours, trying to get her to give herself up and not go through with killing herself and her husband, who was in the house with her.

How did she do it for hours on end? Quinn had asked himself that question every hour since the hostage situation had started.

Her voice still sounded calm and steady even though the last time he had gotten a glimpse of her, dark circles under her eyes accentuated the toll this incident was having on her. He wanted to help her and knew there was nothing he could do but be here when it was over—

which, from what had transpired the past half hour, might be soon. He'd heard Becca's laugh a few minutes ago as she'd joked with the woman, Shelly Roberts.

Becca turned slightly, saying something into the phone headset, and glanced back at him. She gave him a weary smile. He returned it, wishing he could hold her and take some of her stress away.

Becca's heartbeat responded to Quinn's grin by quickening. For a second she didn't hear what Shelly had answered to her question. She twisted around, keeping her gaze trained forward. She couldn't afford to lose her concentration.

"The jerk is having an affair with a friend! I caught them in bed together. Here! The bed I sleep in!"

The woman's voice swung back to hysteria. Over the past hours she had gone from rage to joking to agitation. "I understand. You sound angry at your husband for having an affair."

"He needs to suffer for what he did. I'm gonna make him pay."

Becca knew from the neighbors who had been interviewed that the Roberts family had a gun collection in the house. From what Shelly had said earlier in their conversation she was sure that the woman had one in her hand. "Shelly, why don't you come out here, and we can talk about some solutions to your problem."

Silence.

"Shelly?"

Sobs echoed through the earpiece. "Why doesn't he love me? He'd miss me if I went away."

"What do you mean if you went away, Shelly?"

Becca heard a man yelling in the background. Great. The victim wasn't helping the situation by telling the woman she needed to lose weight.

"If I kill myself, he won't have anyone to take care of him, clean his house, cook his meals," the woman said between bouts of crying.

"Shelly, do you really want to die?"

Again silence filled the phone line. Even though the air was chilly for a summer night, sweat popped out on Becca's forehead and upper lip. She swiped her hand across her brow, then closed her eyes, pinching the bridge of her nose. Tension held her rigid.

"Becca, I'm fine. Just give me a moment. Everything will work out."

The calm in the woman's voice signified a change in the situation. Becca shot to her feet, looking over the barricade that protected her from any stray bullets from the house.

Becca cupped the mouthpiece. "Sarge, I think she's gonna kill herself and her husband. We've got to—"

Through the earpiece she heard a man yell, "No. Don't do it!"

"Move," Becca said as the blast of a weapon echoed through the air.

Too late, she thought, bracing herself for another shot.

Sarge signaled for the tactical team to breach the house. As the members hurried forward, another gunshot sounded over the phone, followed by a scream. Then silence. Thirty seconds passed, and all she heard over the still-open phone line was the police officers moving through the rooms. She ripped off her headset and started for the house as the signal came that the place was secured.

Her heart beat painfully in her chest, and an uncomfortable sensation lodged itself between her shoulder blades. As she moved through the entrance, she smelled gunpowder and blood and knew no good had come from this captive-victim situation.

In the bedroom Becca viewed the slightly overweight woman sprawled on the floor before the full-length mirror that was shattered from a bullet. Shelly had shot herself in the head while her husband sat on the bed, his face buried in his hands, his body shuddering. His cries reverberated in the unearthly quiet.

Shelly had killed herself right after shooting her image in the mirror, and Becca hadn't been able to help the woman. Her failure churned her stomach, the constriction in her chest mushrooming.

"You did all you could, Becca," Sarge said, laying a hand on her shoulder. "At least the victim is alive."

"She was a victim, too." Becca pivoted away from the scene in the bedroom. Already she was beginning to run through the tape in her head, trying to see where she could have altered the outcome of this incident. Later she would review the real tape of the negotiation and maybe have some answers that would help her in the future with other Shellys.

"C'mon. It's been a long night and you still need to do your report, then get some sleep." Sarge walked down the hallway toward the front door.

Becca watched him for a few seconds, then trailed after him. In her mind she knew she couldn't save everyone, that all she could do was her best. But in her heart she felt the loss deeply.

Nearing the command post, Becca saw Quinn and headed toward him, wanting his arms around her, wanting him to tell her everything would be all right. She didn't go into his embrace but stopped a few feet from him, purposely keeping her distance. Someone had switched off a few of the spotlights so a dark pall hung over them. She was glad for that. She didn't want him to see the toll Shelly's death had taken on her. She would work her way through it, but right now she couldn't help but blame herself. There should have been something she could have done to change the situation.

"Becca?"

There was a wealth of concern in that one-worded question. She tried to smile her reassurance, but her mouth wouldn't cooperate. "I'm okay."

"Do you want me to take you home? Or to the station?"

"I'll catch a ride with Sarge back to the station."

"How will you get home?"

"Someone will bring me."

"I can wait for you at the station."

"No, it's been a long night. At least one of us should get some sleep." Because she knew she wouldn't even when she did finally go home.

"Becca, let me—"

She held her palm up. "Quinn, I'll see you later." If she allowed him to comfort her, she might fall apart in front of everyone. The wound of her loss was still too fresh. She needed time.

Quinn watched Becca turn away and climb into a squad car. She was hurting and didn't need him to help her. He realized they hadn't known each other long, but the connection he felt with her was strong—or at least he had thought so. Maybe it was for the best. As he'd witnessed the incident tonight, his fear for her had been reinforced. She laid her life on the line every time she put herself into a hostage situation. Different circumstances from Maggie but the end result was the same. Like Maggie, Becca had a dangerous profession. Could he handle that?

Quinn strode to his truck and left Taylor Street, hoping never to have to return. He started to drive toward his house but found himself parking in Becca's driveway twenty minutes later. He couldn't go home and sleep. And he knew that Becca wouldn't be sleeping anytime soon, either.

Dear Heavenly Father, I want to help Becca. I could see in her expression this hurt her deeply. Please give me the guidance to say and do the right thing for her. She needs You in her life to help her through these tough times.

Although he had a key to Becca's house, he would respect her privacy and not enter without her knowledge. Quinn sat himself on her front porch to wait for her return home. She wouldn't go through it alone if he had anything to say about it. Friends were there for each other through the bad and good times.

Two hours later, as the sun began its journey across the sky, a squad car dropped Becca off in front of her house. The defeated sight of her contracted his heart as though someone had reached into his chest and squeezed it as tight as possible. Not aware of her surroundings, she trudged toward the porch, her shoulders slumped, pain reflected in her expression. He rose from the wicker love seat.

When her gaze fell on him, she ghosted a smile that instantly vanished. "What are you doing here? This is awfully early to start working on the kitchen." She glanced at her watch as though to make sure she had the time right. "You couldn't have gotten more than a few hours sleep."

"I didn't get any. I didn't go home. I've been waiting for you."

The strap of her purse slid off her shoulder and down her arm. She grasped it before her bag dropped to the wooden floor. "Why?"

"I didn't want you to be alone."

His words stirred her, prodding forward the emotions she had held in check. She dared not let go of their tight rein. "Go home to bed, Quinn. I'm going to."

One eyebrow quirked. "Are you?"

"Okay, maybe I'm not gonna go to sleep. Who could after a night like I've had? But I probably should lie down and rest at least. I'm all right. I've lost a person before this incident."

He shuffled forward, his hands in his pockets. "How many?"

"Well, only one other, but I knew when I became a hostage negotiator it could be part of the job."

"Knowing it and experiencing it are two different things."

"Sure, but—" Her throat choked off the rest of her sentence as her pain rose. She hurried toward her front door, hoping to get inside before she fell apart. She contemplated how to shut Quinn out, but before she could, he was in her foyer—large, commanding, a force to be reckoned with.

"It's okay, Becca. You don't have to be strong all the time," he murmured, drawing her to him.

The instant his arms wrapped around her, as though forming a protective shield to keep out the rest of the world, she couldn't hold the tears back. They poured from her as she pressed her cheek against his chest. She cried for all the Shellys of the world, who saw suicide as the only solution to their problems. She cried because she hadn't been able to talk Shelly down, to get her the help she needed. She cried because she couldn't see a relationship with Quinn working out in the long haul. She'd seen the shellshocked expression on his face while watching her deal with the captive-victim situation. When he had time to think about everything, he would compare her job to Maggie's and want nothing to do with her.

Slowly the tears dried, and she managed to put her own battered emotions back in a box deep inside her and lock it. She couldn't afford to indulge in them too much or she wouldn't be able to do her job. And she needed to do her job. For the Shellys of the world.

When he pulled back and framed her face with his large, calloused hands, she relished their rough texture against her skin. It made her feel alive, totally in the moment. Her eyes, burning with exhaustion, focused on his endearing features.

"Thank you," she whispered, her voice husky with the residue of feelings she was wrestling with.

"Why do you do it, Becca?"

"Because someone has to."

"But it doesn't have to be you."

She tugged away. She needed some hot tea, something calming, soothing. She strode toward the kitchen, aware that Quinn was only a foot behind her. He wasn't going to let the issue go.

"Last night I watched the toll that situation demanded of you, Becca. You don't know how many times I wanted to snatch you away and yet you were magnificent hour after hour."

She whirled around in the middle of the chaos that was her kitchen. "I lost her!"

"But you gave one hundred percent. You cared. That's all you could do."

"Yes, I cared about Shelly Roberts. I've seen it too many times in my job—the marriages that break apart because one of the partners is unfaithful. Most, thankfully, don't resort to what Shelly did, but the devastation is just as strong. She could have gotten help to work through her problems. Suicide wasn't the answer." Becca filled her teakettle and put it on the stove to heat. "Do you want any?"

"No. Becca, you didn't answer me. *Why* do you do it?"

After placing a tea bag in a mug, she faced him, pressed against the front of the stove as if she wanted to crawl into the oven and hide. "You know my dad died in a hostage situation. My whole family fell apart after that. I can't let that happen to another family if I can do anything about it. I promised myself that years ago. That's why I went to college. I wanted to be a counselor and try to help people before they got to the end of their rope. The man who killed my father was a bank employee who'd lost his job and didn't see any hope for himself and his family. He flipped out and went crazy, taking several people with him that day."

The shrill sound of the kettle knifed through the tension-laden quiet. Becca turned away from Quinn and prepared her tea, cupping the mug in her cold hands to warm them. Tentatively she took a sip.

"If someone had been there to help that man, my father would be alive today," she said, making her way to the table. Her body trembling with fatigue, she sank down onto the chair, still holding her tea.

"I don't want you to break under this burden you've place on yourself. Let God help you." Quinn came to sit next to her. "With Him by your side, you won't be alone when you face a person in crisis."

"It's not that easy."

"Yes, it is. Let Him into your heart and you'll see. Psalm 46 states it best. God is our refuge and strength, a very present help in trouble."

"Why didn't He help me when I was in need years ago? When my parents died?"

"Maybe He did. He made you strong to weather the pain and do what you needed for your siblings."

Becca shook her head, not sure of that. Yes, she was a strong person most days now. But ten years ago she had floundered and fumbled, making so many mistakes in raising her siblings. She took another long sip, the liquid lukewarm, doing nothing to take the chill away. It burrowed into the marrow of her bones and she couldn't get warm.

Finally, hugging her arms to herself, she murmured, "I don't feel very strong right now."

"I don't know too many people who would after what you went through. You aren't a machine who can turn off your emotions when you want."

"I need to be. Then this wouldn't bother me so much. I'm not gonna last on the hostage negotiation team at this rate." That was another reason why finishing her degree was important. When she could no longer do an effective job as a negotiator, then she would become a counselor as she had dreamed years ago. She would help people in need one way or another.

"Are you always this busy? Two situations in that many weeks?"

"No, not usually. Hopefully this incident today will be the last for a long time." But with Escalante running around, who knew, she thought. The man had been responsible for so many deaths and tragedies.

Quinn seized her gaze and held it. "Will you be okay?"

"I've got to be. I'm due in to work in a few hours."

"Call in sick."

"No! We're checking on the places in Cripple Creek. We have someone watching each one, but we want to find out more from the people in the area. When we make our move, we don't want anything to go wrong. We need to catch Escalante, not give him a chance to get away again."

He covered her hand on the table. "You don't have to do it all. Let Sam do it."

"We're a team. This is too important." She couldn't get it out of her mind that Quinn wasn't safe until Escalante was behind bars. She remembered the slashed tires, a warning he was easy to get to whenever Escalante wanted to.

Quinn scooted back his chair and rose. "Then I'm leaving. Go rest. Sleep if you can." He leaned down and brushed a kiss across her forehead. "I'll be back to work later this morning. I'll let myself out."

She listened to the back door click shut. The sudden silence of the house mocked her. *Yeah, kiss me and then leave. That'll help me get some sleep now.* Exhausted but wide awake, she fixed herself another cup of tea, this one with caffeine, and sat again at the kitchen table.

Lord, if You're listening, please watch out for Quinn. Help me to find Escalante so Quinn doesn't have to look over his shoulder everywhere he goes. Then maybe if I'm not worried about him so much, I can figure out what's going on between us.

After work that evening, Becca felt strange letting herself into Quinn's house. She pocketed his key and headed into his kitchen. Pausing just inside the entrance, she surveyed the neat, orderly room and pictured how hers would look like this soon. Quinn was at her house right now installing her new cabinets.

She crossed to the counter by the refrigerator and placed the sack of groceries on it. She couldn't believe she had actually asked Quinn's mother for a key to his house so she could surprise him with a home-cooked dinner, several days earlier than the Saturday date they had, as a way to thank him for his support after the hostage situation. Fiona had only been too happy to supply the key and a few suggestions on what Quinn liked to eat. She didn't want totally to shock him when he came home because of Escalante's threat, so she had left a note taped to his truck window, telling him she was waiting for him at his house with dinner.

Becca switched on a radio sitting on the counter to a classical station and set about preparing the meal, a pot roast with carrots, potatoes and onions. She also decided to fix a tossed green salad and homemade biscuits. No dessert. The meal was already high calorie, but one of Quinn's favorites.

She finished with the salad and had the biscuits ready to go in at the last minute when her cell phone jingled "Old MacDonald Had a Farm." Checking her caller ID, she frowned. Unknown caller. She clicked it on.

"Hello, Becca."

Her frown deepened. "Who is this?" She was good at recognizing people's voices and this was a stranger, she was sure.

"A friend of the Vances' and Montgomerys'." She could detect a slight accent—a Latino.

She froze, clutching the phone so hard her hand ached. "Why are you calling, Escalante?"

"Just to let you know that Quinn is on his way home. He looked very happy to get your note."

The thudding of her heart thundered in her ears, almost drowning out Escalante's next words.

"You won't stop me. I will win."

Click.

Becca held the cell to her ear for a good minute after Escalante hung up. The menace in the man's voice scared her. He was a killer who wanted Quinn dead. She collapsed back against the counter, gripping its edge to keep herself upright.

What if the properties they were staking out weren't where Escalante was staying? Obviously he was some- where close right now or he wouldn't know about Quinn coming home. She had put her gun in her purse, but decided to strap it back on. After securing it to her waist, she felt better.

She flipped open her cell and called Sam before Quinn arrived. "Escalante just called me. He was watch- ing Quinn at my house, so he's in town right now."

"I'll send some officers over to your street and check it out, but I'm sure he's long gone by now."

"I agree, but he threatened Quinn. In fact, he threat- ened both families. Let's hope one of my neighbors saw something."

"Are you gonna tell Quinn?"

"Yes. He needs to know, but it won't be a surprise. The slashed tires put him on alert."

"Becca, we'll get the man. I'll let you know if the officers find out anything."

Sam's words didn't comfort her because she heard his worried tone. "Nothing from the people watching the properties?"

"You'll be the first to know, I promise. Enjoy your dinner. After last night you deserve a little rest and re- laxation."

"Talk to you later."

Becca released a long sigh as she slid her cell phone into her pocket. "At least I can protect Quinn if Escalante decides to do anything tonight," she murmured to the silent room.

The slamming of a vehicle's door announced Quinn's arrival. She scanned the kitchen, checking to make sure everything was ready. The roast and vegetables were in the oven, their aroma lacing the air with titillating smells. When the back door opened, she pasted a smile on her face and turned toward him.

"After the past twenty-four hours I can't think of anything better to come home to than you cooking dinner for me." Quinn crossed the room and drew her into his arms, kissing her soundly before placing her away from him. He inhaled deeply. "Hmm. If I hadn't been starving, I am now. It smells delicious."

"One of your favorites."

He breathed in another lungful. "Ah, pot roast. How did you know?"

"Your mother. I went to see her today."

"You are indeed a brave woman. Let me wash up and I'll help you."

"No, this is my treat. If my kitchen wasn't all torn up, I'd have cooked this at my house."

Quinn stepped to the sink and lathered up his hands, then rinsed them. "So what should I do?"

She gestured toward his already-set table. "Have a seat. Keep me entertained while I finish up."

He folded his long length into a chair. "With everything that's been happening I forgot to mention that you and I need to go to the tile store. I want you to pick out what you want for a countertop to go with the wallpaper you selected a few days ago. How about first thing tomorrow morning?"

Becca thought of all that needed to be done at work, but Quinn had insisted she have some input into her kitchen. He had told her he didn't do carte blanche. "Is eight too early?"

"Nope. I'll pick you up and we'll go together." He rolled his shoulders and stretched. "When's dinner?"

"Twenty minutes. I have to put the biscuits into the oven. Why, other than the fact that you're *starved?*"

"I thought I would show you my workshop out back if we had the time."

Hot air blasted her face when she opened the oven and stuck the pan of biscuits inside. "Give me a few minutes." She mixed up some spices and sugar with oil and vinegar, then put the bottle into the refrigerator.

"I'm getting the full treatment. You even made salad dressing. I'm impressed."

She spun around, saying, "Nothing but the best for you. I really appreciated your support this morning. I know I need to protect myself from getting too emotionally involved, but for some reason Shelly got to me."

"Are you okay now?" Quinn pinned her with a probing look as he rose from the chair.

"No, but I'm getting there. I listened to part of the tapes today and couldn't see what else I could have done to change the situation."

"Sometimes there's nothing we can do."

"It's in God's hands?"

"Yes." He held out his hand to her. "C'mon. I want to show you my favorite place here."

"A man and his tools and cars."

"At least tools don't cost as much as cars."

Quinn went outside and crossed his yard to a building along the back of his property. When Becca entered his workshop, the scent of sawdust, oil and turpentine wafted in the air. Some tools hung along one wall while a big chest with narrow drawers housed the smaller items. Several workbenches, one with a jigsaw, ran down the middle of the building. Off to one side was a half-finished table that could seat six comfortably.

She walked to it and ran her hand along its smooth surface. "Is this your latest project?"

"Yes, but I've been working on it for over three months. I started it right before the fire at Montgomery Construction. I haven't had much time to finish it."

Tingles flowed down the length of her back as he approached her from behind and put his hands at her waist. His breath fanned her neck and goose bumps rose on her arms.

"I'd kiss you, but any lady armed with a gun gives me second thoughts."

She needed to tell him about the phone call, and his teasing remark was the perfect opening. She angled around so she faced him and suddenly realized her mistake. The table trapped her against him, and all she could think about was his charming smile that could melt a glacier and his nearness that would be her undoing.

"Should I dare take the chance?" Mischief gleamed in his eyes.

"You gonna let a little ol' gun stand in your way," she said with a mock Southern drawl.

"Lady, that ain't any little ol' gun."

Tell him. But his lips were dangerously close, sending her heart rate sky-high. She locked her arms around his neck and boldly ended the taunting play between them by kissing him full on the mouth. After all, she was a take-charge kind of woman. At least that was what she was telling herself as she savored the feel of his lips moving over hers.

When he pulled back slightly, his breathing ragged, he touched her forehead with his, his grasp on her waist tightening. "This is a first."

She leaned back and peered up at him. "What?"

"Kissing in my workshop. In fact, I don't recall any other woman being in here."

She grinned, feeling so totally special and feminine in that moment. "I'm honored." She needed to put a halt to this or she would be kissing him again. Glancing around him, she asked, "Who are you making that table for?"

"You."

"Me?"

"Yours won't fit your new kitchen."

Words failed her. She tried to put two of them together, but all she could think of was that he was personally making her a piece of furniture—a beautifully carved piece that would be in one of her favorite rooms in the house.

"I want to match the finish to the new cabinets. Okay?"

She nodded, still stunned by his gesture. She did things for others, not the reverse.

"Good. Now let's go eat."

"Eat!" She checked her watch and realized if she didn't get into the kitchen fast the biscuits would be burned.

She rushed from the workshop and hurried toward the back door. When she opened the oven to remove the food, she sighed. The biscuits were a little browner than she wished, but not anywhere near being charred.

Having already set the table, she waved Quinn to it, then served the dinner. He ladled his plate with the pot roast, baked vegetables and two biscuits, slathered in butter.

While scooping the salad onto the smaller plate next to his big one, he said, "I could get use to this."

"If I ate like this every day, I would be packing on the pounds." Becca sprinkled some dressing over her greens. "I haven't cooked like this in ages. Even when my siblings lived at home, I didn't have this kind of time to spend cooking."

"Now I'm the one who is honored."

"My captain took one look at me when I dragged myself into work and told me to cut the day short. Sam agreed with him."

He caught her look. "You should be home sleeping."

"I'm a night owl. I can't imagine going to bed before the sun goes down."

"I love working late into the night in my workshop."

Becca thought of the isolation of the building. She hadn't remembered seeing any phone in it, either. "Do me a favor? Don't work out there until Escalante is caught."

A frown wrinkled his brow. "I'm not letting that man rule my life."

Tell him. "He called me on my cell this evening."

Quinn stared at Becca, sitting at his kitchen table, but all he saw was red—his company buildings going up in flames, the blood of Escalante's victims. Quinn gripped the fork he had been bringing to his mouth tightly until the metal bit into his palm. Becca's beautiful face came back into focus.

"Why?" he finally managed to ask between gritted teeth.

"To inform me he knows what you and I are doing this evening."

"How?"

"Because he read the note I taped to your truck."

"He was at the house again!" Quinn bolted to his feet, his hands fisted.

"He's taunting me—the police—because we haven't found him."

Quinn tightened his hands even more, his knuckles white. For a few seconds he welcomed the pain, centered his thoughts on it. He wanted to punch something—preferably Escalante's face. Instead, he slowly uncurled his fists and turned from the table to pace the length of his kitchen. "Is that why you're wearing your gun?"

"Yes. I debated whether to tell you or not. But you have a right to know and to take the appropriate actions."

"And what are they?" His long strides chewed up the space between them. He hovered over her.

"Watch your back. Don't take any unnecessary risks. Be careful where you go. Lock your doors—"

"In other words, hide. Or, better yet, I could just leave town until you catch him."

She rose to meet his direct look. "That might not be such a bad idea."

"Well, I'm not gonna do that. Let him come after me." Quinn knew the foolishness of that declaration—Escalante was a dangerous killer—but all he wanted to do was come face-to-face with the man and make him pay for all the misery he'd caused his family.

"Oh, good! Why don't you just pin a target on your chest?"

He met her glare for glare. "If that's what it takes, I would. This can't continue."

Her stiff stance melted, and she sank onto her chair. "I shouldn't have said anything until later. Escalante has managed to ruin this evening. There's no stopping what that man can do even when he's not around."

Quinn, still towering over her, scanned the table, the food lovingly prepared by Becca's hands, the bouquet of daisies in a vase in the middle. Their cheerful yellow color mocked him.

He collapsed into the chair next to Becca. "I'm sorry. I overreacted. I'd blame it on the lack of sleep, but I'd be lying. My life has been so disrupted for the past few months because of Escalante. To think he has deliberately targeted you was just too much."

Becca grasped his hand nearest her, cupping both hers around his. "He wants to rattle my cage."

"Has he?" Losing concentration because of Escalante's ploy could be dangerous for her.

"I'm concerned. I'd be a fool not to be. But by contacting me he could make a mistake. He's getting bold slashing tires, taunting the police. He thinks he's invincible. He isn't. I've dealt with criminals like him before and that can be their downfall."

Although his stomach constricted in a huge lump, he glanced at his plate full of delicious food and said, "Let's finish. I don't want all your hard work to go to waste."

She released his hand and turned to her meal. "The one good thing about this dinner is that it can easily be reheated."

He chuckled. "Who gets the leftovers, you or me?"

"I like the tile you picked out for your countertop," Quinn said as he drove out of the store's parking lot.

To be honest, Becca hadn't put much thought into her selection. All that was on her mind was the fact that the officers who had talked to her neighbors had come up with a report of a black Jeep Cherokee seen parked on her street around the time she'd left the note with a vague description of a dark-haired man sitting in its front seat as if waiting on someone. It had to be Escalante. Driving a black Jeep.

"Becca?"

The question in Quinn's voice pulled her away from her thoughts. "Yes?"

"You haven't said two words since I picked you up."

"Yes, I have."

He gave her an exasperating glance. "You know what I mean. Something up with the case?"

She sighed, not wanting to keep anything from Quinn

that might save his life. "A black Jeep Cherokee was seen on my street about the time I left the note on your truck."

"So you think that's what Escalante is driving."

"Yes. At least I hope so. It will help us in our search."

Quinn peered at the rearview mirror. "Then I think Escalante is following us."

Becca swiveled around and stared out the back window. Sure enough, several cars back was a black Jeep. Excitement gripped her. She fumbled for her cell and placed a call to Sam, reporting the vehicle behind them.

As she flipped her phone close, Quinn swerved across a lane of traffic and made a sharp turn to the right. "What are you doing?"

"Seeing if that's Escalante."

Becca's mouth hung open for a few seconds before she snapped it closed and followed the line of traffic behind them in the side mirror. The black Jeep made the same turn and was now a hundred feet behind them. When Quinn sped up, so did the Jeep. Quinn flew down several back streets while Becca was on the phone again to inform Sam of this recent development. As she was giving her partner their latest location, the vehicle behind them decelerated, then turned at the next intersection.

Quinn tightened his grasp on the steering wheel, slowed and made a U-turn. "He isn't getting away from us."

He headed for the street that the Jeep had just taken. Becca grabbed her gun from her waist, wanting to be prepared in case they caught whoever had been following them.

As they headed up into the mountains toward Cripple Creek, the winding road underscored the danger in this pursuit. Quinn shouldn't be involved, and yet Becca knew he would never halt until they either lost the Jeep or stopped it. The sheer determination in his expression reflected how she felt, and she understood what was going through Quinn right now. His family had been threatened—as he had—and he wasn't going to let Escalante get away.

NINE

The screech of the tires as Quinn sped around a curve filled the truck. Becca's hand on the door handle tightened, and she gritted her teeth so hard that her whole jaw ached.

"Where's the backup?" Quinn asked as he maneuvered another sharp series of curves.

"Coming." Becca peered behind them and saw a glimpse of a black-and-white not far away.

The hard planes of Quinn's face emphasized the intense concentration it took to stay on the mountain road. Becca stared out the side window at the sheer drop hundreds of feet into the tops of a forest of trees.

The truck hugged the shoulder dangerously close to the edge. *Lord, help us.* Becca said the prayer over and over as they took one bend in the road after another, trying to keep the black Jeep in sight.

On a straightaway Quinn gunned his truck, his tires chewing up the asphalt. Becca kept her gaze trained on the road up ahead as it climbed upward, trying to find the Jeep. It couldn't be that far in front of them, but it was nowhere to be seen. Two squad cars roared up behind them.

"I think we've lost him," Becca finally said as they began their ascent.

"No, I'm not giving up. He couldn't have just vanished."

"Maybe one of the turnoffs we went by?"

The truck slowed. Frowning, Quinn glanced down at his instrument panel. "I'm out of gas. I just filled up. I don't understand." He steered the truck toward a turnout and came to a halt.

One of the black-and-whites raced on by while the other stopped. Becca and Quinn clambered from the truck and met the officer halfway between the two vehicles.

"Is there a problem?" the police office asked.

Quinn squatted down and examined the underside of his truck. "Yeah, my gas tank has a leak in it."

Becca inspected where Quinn pointed. "I don't believe in coincidences."

"Neither do I. Escalante wanted us to follow him for a short time. He's enjoying taunting us."

Sam pulled up in his car a few minutes later after Quinn had placed a call to his auto club. Becca had sent the other squad car on to keep looking for the black Jeep. She gave the officer her cell number in case he discovered anything.

When Sam joined them by the mountain road, he said, "So far the officers haven't found anything. We're going to start searching all the side roads off this one from here back."

"Isn't one of the properties we're interested in along

this road?" Becca shielded her eyes against the glare of the sun.

"That's the first place we'll visit." Sam turned to Quinn. "Can you wait by yourself for the tow truck? I need Becca to come with me."

"I can't talk you into letting me tag along?"

Becca said no at the same time as Sam did.

Quinn's fierce features stressed his displeasure at their answer. "If it hadn't been for me, you wouldn't have this lead."

"And we appreciate it. But, Quinn, you have to let Becca and me do our job without worrying about a civilian getting caught up in a shootout."

"Shootout," Quinn murmured, a closed expression descending.

Becca knew what was going through his mind in that exact moment. He was thinking about Maggie's death and comparing her and his dead fiancée's jobs.

"So I'm supposed to go about my day as though nothing is happening?" Quinn stood in front of her, blocking her path.

"Yes. Let me do my job. I'm good at it. We'll find Escalante. His boldness may be his downfall."

"I'll have my cell. I'll be at your house working after I get my truck towed. Please keep me informed or…" His voice thickened. He averted his gaze for a few seconds, then directed the full impact of his look into her eyes. "Be careful."

Hidden in a line of trees later that same day, Becca spied the cabin through binoculars with the black Jeep parked around back. No movement. Based on Alessandro's description, the two officers staking out the property thought Escalante was inside. She felt in her gut they were right. To make everything legal and aboveboard, Sam was securing a search warrant before they went in. This gave them time to arrange everything. Slowly the tactical team was moving into place, surrounding the cabin, setting up a perimeter.

Sunlight streamed down through the branches of the aspen and pines, heating the back of her neck. Sweat beaded on her forehead. Even in the cooler mountain air, the day was hotter than usual. Was it an omen?

She itched to end this once and for all. But so much of police work required patience and the ability to wait. Keeping the binoculars trained on the front of the cabin, she thought back to the night before with Quinn at his house. She'd been so tempted to ask him if she could stay to protect him from Escalante. She didn't. But when she'd left, she'd worried the whole way home about him being alone with that monster running loose. The first thing she'd done when she'd entered her house was call him to make sure he was still all right.

He hadn't said anything about her unexpected call, but she had known he realized why she had phoned him. Hanging up, she had sat for a long time, staring into space. Then it had hit her. She had fallen in love with Quinn and that wasn't going to go away. The feeling had thrilled and frightened her—still did. How had it happened so quickly? She'd dated Sam a long time and had never felt that way about him.

"I've got it," Sam said, slipping in next to her. He patted his pocket.

The few windows there were in the cabin were covered, giving no visual into the place. The snipers were situated with their guns ready if needed.

"Command has decided we're moving in." Sam shifted next to Becca, getting more comfortable as they waited. "They don't think Escalante knows we're out here. We'll wait until after they have secured the place."

"I'm not so sure about that," Becca said, the feeling in her gut intensifying. But the SWAT team knew the risk and had decided this was the best course of action. Time would tell.

Becca watched as the tactical team ran forward in a crouch toward the cabin, maneuvering themselves yard by yard closer to the log structure, hiding behind whatever cover there was—an old rusty car, a pine tree, a bush. Swinging the binoculars toward the front facade, she saw the barrel of a rifle appear in one of the two windows at the same time as several shots were fired at the members of the team, sending dirt flying at their feet. A bullet hit one officer in the leg. Sanders collapsed to the ground, dragging himself behind a tree. He was now pinned down.

"He knew," Sam muttered.

It made sense, Becca thought, following the SWAT team's retreat, checking on the wounded officer, who gave a thumbs-up sign while he pressed his hand into his thigh. Sanders would need help soon. Time was running out. "We've been out here in full force for half an hour, assessing the situation, getting into place. If I was a killer, running for my life, I would be checking the terrain every so often, especially when we gave chase earlier this morning."

"I guess we'll go to Plan B. Negotiating."

The knot in her stomach blossomed, seemingly taking over her whole body. Escalante wanted the man she loved to pay with his death. The fallen officer could bleed to death if not rescued soon. So much was at stake. She had to do what she could. "There's a phone line into the cabin. Does anyone know the number?"

Sam withdrew his notepad and read it off. "I'll be back in a sec. I'll check in with command to see if this is what they want to do next."

Situated a hundred and fifty yards away, dressed in her body armor and mostly protected by the cover of a ridge, Becca felt relatively safe, but sweat still encased her. This could be a long siege. She couldn't picture Escalante walking out on his own.

"Make the call," Sam said, coming back. "They're willing to try negotiating while they come up with another plan. Sanders won't last long."

Becca punched in the numbers and waited while it rang. When someone picked up but didn't say anything, she went into her spiel. "This is Becca Hilliard with the Colorado Springs Police Department. We have a warrant for your arrest, Escalante. We are not leaving here without you." She shifted to get a better view on the cabin to see if there was any activity.

Heavy breathing sounded through the line, then a deep, gravelly voice said, "You won't take me alive. I have nothing to lose."

At the same time as she heard a shot she felt something pierce through her body armor. For a few seconds she didn't realize what had happened, then she looked down and saw the hole in her armor. Pain spread through her left shoulder, causing her to drop her phone. She sank against the ridge, the grass pressed into her right cheek.

From the cell next to her, she heard Escalante's laugh. "That one is for Quinn." Then the phone connection was severed.

Sam was at her side, hunched low. "He has armor-piercing bullets!"

She gave her partner a weak smile. "So it would seem."

"Got to get you out of here." Sam scanned the area, but a frown furrowed his forehead. "I can't risk moving you back behind the outer perimeter. Not only does he have armor-piercing bullets, he shoots like a sniper. We're all pinned down."

Pain clouded her mind as she compressed her right hand over the wound. Blood oozed between her fingers. "Then I've got to try to get him out of the cabin." Light-headed, she tried to lift her cell, but Sam stopped her.

"You heard him." He took the phone. "I'll call—"

An explosion rocked the ground, a deafening sound seemed to suck the air away. Becca inched up to see the cabin engulfed in flames, a column of black smoke billowing into the sky.

"He blew himself up," she gasped, the vision of the fire spinning before her eyes.

* * *

Escalante had followed them this morning! Tampered with his gas tank!

Quinn pounded the nail in with more force than was needed, but he had to do something to rid himself of the anger inside. Escalante was dragging Becca into the middle of his plot to seek revenge against the two families. And Quinn's feelings were the reason why. Somehow the man had seen what Quinn had been trying to deny to himself, to others. He was falling in love with Becca and he shouldn't. The reasons it wouldn't work between them were still there and now Becca was in danger.

Being surrounded by Becca's things made his resolve to put some distance between them waver. On the desk across the kitchen sat a picture of her and her siblings. Glancing back at it, he zeroed in on her huge smile, which dominated the photo. His pulse rate sped as his truck had earlier this morning when Escalante was within his reach. Yeah, he was gonna back off, Quinn thought sarcastically.

Taking a survey of the half-finished room, with part of the cabinets in and part not, he laughed, no humor in the sound. Working for the lady was going to make it difficult. At least she was usually at work. He would just have to make a point to be long gone by the time she was due home. No more waiting around for her to appear. No more dinners—well, after the rehearsal dinner next week since he'd already invited her.

Yep, when Colleen's wedding was over, he would hurry and complete the renovation project in record time. After all, he had a lot of work at Montgomery

Construction that needed his attention. His dad could go back into retirement. He could take over the hospital wing's construction.

But then you can't do what you love best, a little voice sounded off in his mind. Okay, so he liked renovation projects. He'd just have to find another one with a little old lady who didn't look like dynamite in a sundress, in a navy blue pantsuit.

He started to pound another nail when his cell buzzed. Putting his hammer on the counter, he flipped open his phone and practically growled, "Montgomery here."

"Quinn, this is Sam."

The urgency in his friend's voice alerted Quinn, drawing him up. "Yeah?"

"Becca is on the way to Vance Memorial. She was shot while we were closing in on Escalante."

"How bad?" His grip on his phone threatened to snap it in two.

"She's lost a lot of blood. Not sure."

"I'm on my way," Quinn said, striding toward the back door while he talked.

He closed his cell and stuffed it into the front pocket of his jeans. Quickening his step, he rounded Becca's house and climbed into his truck. Fumbling to insert his key, he dropped it. The pounding of his heart thundered in his mind as though a hammer was striking against his skull. For a few seconds his vision blurred, and he groped for the key chain. Finally the haze cleared and he snatched it up and started the truck.

Please, Lord, don't take Becca away. I can't lose another one. Please watch over her and take care of her.

* * *

Seated next to Becca's hospital bed in the dim light, Quinn waited for her to wake up. After the surgery to repair her shoulder, she'd been sleeping off the effects of the anesthesia, giving him time to do a lot of thinking. None of it good. Even though Escalante was dead from the explosion, that didn't mean there wouldn't be another time that Becca's life would be placed in jeopardy. She was a homicide detective and on the negotiation team for the department, both dangerous assignments—like the bomb squad.

"Son?"

Quinn jerked his head up and looked toward the door. "Dad, what are you doing here?"

"Checking on Becca and you. How's she doing?" Leaning heavily on his cane, his father moved farther into the room until he stood at the end of the bed.

"She should be fine. No permanent damage—this time."

Joe quirked an eyebrow. "Meaning?"

"What about next time?"

"You're thinking about Maggie."

"Wouldn't you?"

"Not the same, son."

Quinn buried his face in his hands, slowly scrubbing them down it. "I can't do this a second time."

His father came to his side and grasped his shoulder. "Put your trust in the Lord, Quinn. Someone has to do her job. What will this world become if no one will? We need people like her."

"I'm not asking her to give up her job for me. I

couldn't do that. No one is happy if they are forced to make a choice like that. But I can't love someone whose life is on the line every day."

"Everyone's life is on the line every day. When it's our time, it's our time, son. Besides, we don't always have control over who we fall in love with."

"Well, I do." *Yeah, right,* an inner voice countered. *Who are you fooling?*

Quinn set his jaw, refusing to get into a debate with his father over this issue. He was just too tired to make any sense. The pressure of his dad's hold on his shoulder increased for a few seconds before he released it and sat on the small couch along the wall.

"There's no reason for you to lose sleep, too, Dad."

"In other words, go home."

Quinn nodded, wanting to be alone to grapple with his conflicting emotions that were colliding with each other. He wanted to hold her, to take her suffering away, and yet that would only prolong the inevitable—him backing off.

His father headed for the door. "I'm only a phone call away."

When the door swished closed, Quinn took a deep, fortifying breath. Part of him couldn't forget that Becca was lying in this hospital bed because of him. If Escalante hadn't wanted to hurt him, hadn't taunted them this morning, she wouldn't have been shot.

Quinn bowed his head and began a series of prayers, alternating between asking God to protect Becca and to help him walk away from her when the time came. He wouldn't when she needed him. She was hurt because of him, and he would be there for her through her recovery. He owed her that. But after that—

"Quinn?"

Her weak, raspy voice pulled his attention to her face, pale with dark circles accentuating her pain-filled eyes. His heart slowed to a throb. If he could bear her pain, he would in a heartbeat.

He scooted forward. "I'm right here. How are you doing?"

She moved so she could see him better and winced. "Lousy. Is Escalante dead?"

"Yep. They found a charred body in the rubble of the burned-out cabin. They're checking DNA to see if it's Escalante, but it fits the description of height. Besides, where could he have gone? There was only one door in and you all had him surrounded."

She sighed. "It's over. Then it was worth it." Her eyes slid close for a few seconds. When she peered at him again, she licked her lips and asked, "Can I have a drink of water?"

Her weak voice and pale features tore at his heart. He turned toward the bedside table and poured a glass, his hold on the pitcher shaky. When he finally got control of his nerves, he helped her drink by holding her up, careful of her bandaged shoulder. When he touched her, his throat closed. He had almost lost her.

She rested her head back on the pillow, again her eyes shutting. "How'd they get Escalante's DNA?"

"Peter's son, Manuel."

"You know?"

"I do now. Manuel is Escalante's son. But it will take some time to verify that the body is Escalante."

"Good. I don't want there to be any doubts this time. It'll put closure on this own thing. I'm glad…." Her voice faded into silence as sleep overcame her.

Quinn observed her for a few minutes, then rose to work the kinks out. After stretching and rolling his head, he strode to the door. He needed a strong cup of coffee. It would be a long night.

Stepping off the elevator, Quinn made his way to the cafeteria and purchased a large coffee. As he started to leave, Jake Montgomery came into the room.

"What are you doing here?" Quinn asked.

"I could ask you the same thing, but I heard about Becca and what happened at the cabin with Escalante. I'm here because Holly went into premature labor. The doctor has stopped it, but wants to keep her overnight. Run some tests."

"I'm sorry to hear that. I know she had a scare a while back."

"Yeah, but I think everything will be all right." Jake walked to the counter and filled himself a large cup of coffee, then rejoined Quinn by the door. "We only have a few more months to go."

"I'll stop by and give Holly my support. She's family and if she needs anything, just let me know."

On the elevator ride, Jake asked, "How's Becca doing?"

"Okay. She should go home tomorrow or the next day."

"That's great. Are you bringing her to Colleen's wedding?"

"Yes."

"We'll be able to celebrate more than my sister's wedding. Escalante's dead. Holly should be all right with bed rest. Life is good."

Quinn wished he felt that way, but right now he was faced with a lonely life. Becca had given him a glimpse of what he was missing. He wanted to be married. He wanted a family. He had grown up around a large, loving family and knew the importance of having one.

When Quinn walked by the nursery with Jake and glanced inside at all the bassinets with babies in them, emotions he'd tried to bury swelled. He wanted a child, a wife, a family of his own.

Becca stared out the window at the bright June day, the Rockies in the background. She was finally alone after a steady stream of visitors this morning. When she had opened her eyes earlier, she'd found Quinn slumped in the chair next to her hospital bed, sound asleep. The sight of him had made her realize she would have done the day before all over again if it meant the threat to his life was gone. For a few seconds she didn't disguise the love she felt for him. She felt it pouring from her heart and her expression.

Lord, if You're listening, thank You for protecting Quinn and keeping him safe from Escalante.

He'd left an hour ago to get some rest, telling her he would be back to bring her home from the hospital.

Dr. Adam Montgomery came into the room, his blue eyes gleaming with a smile. "I hear you're demanding to go home this afternoon."

"Too many visitors. It seems everyone came to make sure Holly was all right and decided to stop by and thank me for helping to end Escalante's reign of terror."

"And like you, Holly's screaming to go home." Adam checked his handiwork on her shoulder. "This shouldn't affect your range of motion. Give it a few weeks before playing on the police department's softball team."

"I'll keep your advice in mind."

"No work for at least a week."

"Can I at least work the desk at the station?" She couldn't imagine sitting around and resting for a whole week. She'd never done that.

"I want to see you in a week and I'll let you know if you can."

"You doctors are such tyrants," Becca said with a laugh.

"That's what they pay us the big bucks for." Adam headed for the door, paused and glanced back. "I want to add my thanks to all the rest of the Montgomerys'."

Quinn was so lucky to have such a large family that knew what the word "family" truly meant. She only had her brother and sister. Although both had wanted to come home to make sure she was all right, she had insisted they stay where they were. She had known it wouldn't have been easy for either one to leave their jobs and school when she'd only suffered a minor wound. Well, maybe not minor but she was determined not to let it get her down for long.

Her door opened again and in walked Sam. She grinned. "I was just thinking about you. What brings you by? Holly?"

He sent her an exasperated glance. "You're the reason I'm here. I just finished all the paperwork on the incident yesterday. I tell you, some officers will go to great lengths not to fill out paperwork, even getting shot."

The teasing in his voice made her smile grow. "You're just jealous I thought of it before you."

Sam sat in the same chair Quinn had vacated earlier. "Seriously, are you all right?"

"Almost as good as new."

"After you came out of surgery, and I had to go to the station, Quinn kept me informed."

"So you were with Quinn while I was in the O.R.?"

"Yeah."

"How did he seem to you?" Although Quinn had said all the right things when she had awakened, a shadow had clouded his eyes and there had been a certain reservation about him.

"What do you think? He was worried. He spent a good part of the time in the chapel praying for you or pacing around the waiting room until I wanted to scream."

"Did he say anything about Maggie?"

"Why would he?" Sam's expression brightened. "You're worried that Quinn will think your shooting was like what happened to Maggie?"

She nodded.

"It's not the same. Being on the bomb squad puts you in danger every time you're called out to defuse a bomb. There was nothing in Escalante's dossier that indicated the man knew how to shoot like a sniper. You had on body armor and should have been a safe enough distance from the cabin."

She knew all that. But still, would that make a difference to Quinn when he began to think about it? If he hadn't already, he would.

"You worry too much, Becca. I'm glad you're dating Quinn. He's a good man." Sam rose. "I'd better go see Holly before I leave here. I'll talk to you later. Enjoy your time off."

Time off? Becca hadn't taken much, and now she would be stuck at home for at least a week. The bright spot of the whole situation was that Quinn would be working there and finishing up her kitchen. That realization brought a smile to her lips. Maybe it wouldn't be so bad.

Not fifteen minutes later another member of the Montgomery and Vance families entered her room. An orderly wheeled Holly inside and parked her by the bed, then left.

"I'm hiding out," Holly said with a wink. "I'm gonna have to go home to get the rest the doctor has prescribed for me. I've seen relatives I haven't seen in—" she fluttered her hand in the air "—in at least a week."

The light laughter that accompanied Holly's words produced Becca's own. "Well, this isn't the place to be. Frankly I didn't know there were so many family members."

"I've come to add my thanks to all the others'." Holly moved her wheelchair closer and shifted to get more comfortable. Then her eyes grew round and she splayed her hand over her round stomach. "This sucker is an active one. Here, you want to feel? Either he's doing a victory dance or she's doing some kind of gymnastics routine."

Becca laid her palm where Holly indicated and felt the jab. She smiled. What a wondrous sensation! To feel your baby growing inside you. Emotion swelled up inside Becca. That was one part of motherhood she hadn't experienced.

Okay, now Becca *knew* something was wrong. She'd been holed up in the house for three days and hadn't seen Quinn much at all—unless she counted the times he was surrounded by several men furiously working to complete the kitchen. The hole in the attic was patched, and when she walked into the third bedroom, she couldn't even tell that she'd fallen through the ceiling.

Quinn left with the rest of the men. He never lingered to talk. When they did exchange words, they were polite but held a certain distance. She wasn't sure what to do about the situation. She wasn't good at dating, not having done a lot in the past, with all her family and work demands.

Becca dragged herself out of her bed and slipped on her slippers. Napping in the middle of the day was so uncharacteristic of her, but she was so tired after being up for a few hours that if she didn't lie down she would never make it to five o'clock. And she definitely wasn't going to bed at five in the afternoon!

Sounds from the kitchen had died as she padded down the hall toward it. It wouldn't be long before

Quinn refurbished its hardwood floor, the last item to be done. Then would he be gone for good?

She pushed open the door and entered the room to find Quinn measuring the space where the countertop had been. There was no one else in the kitchen. She'd been silent, but he whirled around, as though he felt her look drill into his back, and locked gazes with her.

"You didn't sleep long," he said, turning back to his work.

"Is that why you're alone? You didn't expect me to be up so soon?" she asked, deciding not to skirt the issue that had been plaguing her for days.

He stiffened. "My men are taking a late lunch."

She walked toward him. "Haven't you eaten?"

"Not yet. Mom insisted on bringing by something for me to eat—and you." His head bowed, he marked off some spaces on a piece of wood.

"She did? How sweet."

"Sweet." He chuckled. "You know what she's up to?"

"Yeah, she's not too hard to figure out." Becca relaxed next to him, leaning against the cabinets with a gaping hole where the counter should be. Quinn, on the other hand, wasn't as easy to read.

"I put her off for the past several days. I know how wiped out you've been. I ran out of excuses this morning. Be prepared for a banquet."

How sweet, Becca thought again. Maybe he was only being considerate of her sleeping all the time and not wanting to disturb her rest. "When should she be here?"

"Probably not for another hour. I thought you would sleep longer." He slanted a look toward her as he moved down the counter away from her.

Something she wasn't quite sure of filled his gaze before he masked it. Pain? Regret? Becca rubbed her hands down her face, exhaustion still clinging to her mind. She couldn't even read a person clearly, which was one of her assets as a police officer.

"I told her to come around to the back door. I'll let you know when the food is here."

She was being dismissed.

Her expression must have reflected her thoughts because he added, "I need to finish this before the men get back so we can complete the counters today."

"So in other words, get lost," she said in a teasing tone, but deep down she hurt, because he'd already pulled away emotionally.

TEN

"Jessica, what are you doing here?" Becca said later that afternoon after Quinn and his crew had left.

"Can't a friend come over and see if you're all right?" She came into the foyer, her arms laden with a casserole dish and a bowl of salad. "Quinn said to let you rest for a few days before we started visiting you."

"That's what he told me earlier." Becca closed the front door and followed her friend into the living room.

"He even had us stagger our visits so you wouldn't get so tired."

Stunned, Becca blinked. "So his mother came earlier and you now. Who's next?"

"Let me put this in the kitchen. Be right back." Jessica disappeared for a few minutes and when she re-entered the living room, she took a seat on the couch. "I think Sam's parents are next. They didn't have a chance to thank you yet." She tossed her head toward the kitchen. "Quinn's work is beautiful. I didn't even recognize it as the same room."

"All that's left is the wallpapering and the floors. Then he's done."

"Did you know he pulled some men from other projects to help get it done?"

"No, although I thought more people were here. Why?"

"He didn't want you to be without your kitchen any longer. I think it's one of his ways of telling you thank you."

With her arm in a sling, Becca shifted on the couch, trying to get more comfortable. Her wound continued to be a nagging throb. "I was doing my job. That's all. Sam and others were there."

"And they're getting swamped with thanks, too. I don't think you realize the toll Escalante has had on our two families over the past few years. His reign has finally ended. Praise the Lord!"

"Jessica—" Becca hesitated, not sure how to say what she was feeling. "I've noticed lately that I'm talking to God again. I used to as a child. My father taught me how. He always felt it was like having a conversation with your best friend. But I still have doubts. I—" Her throat jammed; she couldn't finish her sentence, her emotions of late so close to the surface.

"I know. I went through the same thing when I met and fell in love with Sam." She spread her arms wide. "And look where I am today. You'll come to terms with these new feelings." She leaned forward. "I heard you're going with Quinn to Colleen's rehearsal dinner at the end of the week. Do you want some help shopping?"

"Shopping? I hadn't planned on going shopping."

Jessica wrinkled her forehead. "I could bring some

outfits here if you're too tired to go out. I thought we could go Thursday afternoon. That gives you a few more days to rest. Knowing you, you'll be chomping at the bit to get out of this house by then."

"You know me well. I would have already been doing that if I hadn't been sleeping so much. But today I didn't take too many naps so I know I'm getting my energy back."

"Good. Then we'll have lunch and go to a few stores." Jessica stood. "This is gonna be so much fun! We certainly deserve a celebration. We've got so much to be thankful for and it looks like the completion of your kitchen will be another thing to add to the list."

"Do you like it?" Quinn asked in the middle of her newly renovated kitchen on Friday afternoon.

Becca made a full circle, taking in the cherrywood cabinets, light granite countertops, polished hardwood floor, tumbled-marble backsplash and large walk-in pantry concealed behind cabinet doors. "I can't believe it's finished. Just in time for me to go back to work next Monday."

The mention of work brought a frown to Quinn's face. "Are you sure you're all right to go in?"

She slowly moved her left arm, being careful not to do it too quickly. "Good as new, or it will be soon. I'll be on desk duty until my shoulder and arm are one hundred percent, but the nice thing is I don't have to stare at these four walls all day long." *Especially since you won't be here,* she added silently. His presence had been the only bearable part of the past week on house rest—even if she had to make it a point to go into the kitchen to see Quinn.

"And once you're back at work with no restrictions you'll be happy?"

"Of course. I'm the type of person who must keep busy. Didn't you get that point this week when I bothered you every two minutes when I wasn't sleeping?"

His mouth spread into a grin. "I did stumble over you a couple of times while trying to work."

"See," she said in a teasing voice.

"I know what you mean about keeping busy. It has saved me on a number of occasions."

"After Maggie's death?" Becca knew she was treading into dangerous territory that they had avoided all week, but she was never one to run from a problem. She'd discovered hiding from a problem didn't make it go away.

"Yes." Tension vibrated down his length, charging the air.

Suddenly the space between them seemed to grow, when in actuality neither moved. "I'm very good at my job. I don't take unnecessary risks and I've been trained well."

"So was Maggie."

"Life is a risk, Quinn. I could go to the grocery store for a carton of milk and be in a fatal accident. Anyone could, including you."

"So you didn't worry about me one bit while Escalante was running around town slashing my tires, following us?"

"Well, yes. I care about you. I worry about people I care about."

His intense gaze sought hers, drilling into her. "Then you know how I feel." He strode toward the back door. "I'll pick you up at seven tonight for the rehearsal dinner."

As he shut the door, Becca couldn't shake the feeling he was shutting her out of his life bit by bit. Her attempt to reassure him about her job hadn't been successful, and she wasn't sure she ever would be because police work was more dangerous than an ordinary job.

The top two floors of the mayor's mansion, a beautiful bricked structure that used to be the jail, housed the family while the bottom ones were offices for the city government. Becca had never been up to the mayor's residence even though Sam was her partner and his father lived here. She took in the beautifully designed foyer with the living room and large dining room off it. The gleaming chandelier reflecting off the marble floor lit the entry as if the sun shone. The rich dark wood, polished to a high sheen, accentuated the walls, painted a deep burgundy.

She pulled her black lace shawl tighter about her, suddenly feeling as though she had stepped into another world, one of money and power. Seeing all the women in beautiful after-five dresses, she was glad that Jessica had insisted she take her shopping for something to wear. Nothing in her dull wardrobe, geared toward work, would have been appropriate.

But still, she thought, glancing down at her black silk dress that fell to just below her knees and hugged her curves, she wasn't used to wearing something like this.

Her mother's strand of pearls hung around her neck, the only color to her attire.

She turned toward Quinn, who came up behind her, her hair, newly cut, brushing her shoulders. She resisted the urge to suck in a deep breath at the sight of him in a tuxedo. It fit so well it couldn't be a rental, which emphasized he lived in a different world than she. He moved with the ease of a man used to wearing a tuxedo to functions. Whereas her three-inch high heels that Jessica had insisted were perfect for her dress were as alien to her as being comfortable sitting around doing nothing all day.

"How big is the wedding party?" she asked when she caught sight of the crowd gathered in the huge living room obviously constructed with the idea that the mayor would be hosting large parties.

"There are six groomsmen and bridesmaids as well as a best man. Not to mention Amy is the flower girl and Bobby Fletcher is the ring bearer. Colleen declared she was only going to get married once so she intended to do it right." Quinn craned his neck to look into the room. "The whole Vance and Montgomery families are here, including the children."

"Like at the barbecue?"

"Worse. Not everyone was there. I see Michael Vance with his fiancée, Layla Dixon. I see Alessandro's brother, Tomas, too." He put his hand at the small of her back. "Ready? It looks like the party is in full swing."

Becca inhaled deeply at the feel of his fingers on her. Sliding him a sheepish look, she said, "Sorry. I'm not used to dressing up, and with my shoulder still giving me some problems, I didn't realize how long it would take me to get ready."

"No complaint from me. I avoid these fancy kinds of affairs if I can."

"You do? You look so natural in a tux."

"I haven't been very successful in avoiding these kinds of affairs. Since my uncle was mayor before Max, I was expected to go to a lot of galas."

"There you two are. We were wondering where you were," Max said, limping toward them with a welcoming grin on his face. "We started without you. We have much to celebrate tonight."

"So your nephew hasn't backed out at the last minute," Quinn said.

Max laughed. "My wife wouldn't allow it. No, Alessandro is in there, stuck to Colleen's side. You need to meet his little daughter, Mia. Adorable. Now that Escalante is gone, the threat is, too, so they felt it was safe for her to come to the wedding. She is going to stand up there with them."

Wearing a teal blue dress of silk with brocaded flowers and sequins that fell in soft waves to midcalf, Colleen joined them in the foyer. "I thought you'd skipped out on this shindig, cousin."

Quinn checked his watch. "I was fifteen minutes late, and you all were ready to send out the posse?"

"No, we just couldn't start without Becca. She and Sam are the reason we don't have to lock down the church tomorrow like Fort Knox." Colleen embraced Becca. "I'm so glad my cousin has such good taste. Welcome and thank you."

"I guess then there are no hard feelings about being questioned in connection to Neil O'Brien's murder."

"I knew I hadn't done it. It was just a matter of time before you and Sam figured it out."

"We knew, but we had to follow the leads."

Alessandro approached, holding the hand of a little girl with brown hair and eyes like his. Becca knew this was his daughter, Mia, because she looked so much like her father. "Good. Everyone is here now. Quinn, Becca, I want you to meet Mia."

When Mia smiled up at her, staying close to her father, Becca's heart responded. She thought of her sister, Caitlin, at that age and could remember how adorable she had been. For a few seconds a yearning took hold of Becca before she quickly dismissed it. She'd spent half of her life raising her brother and sister.

"Is this the first time you've been in the United States?" Becca asked the child.

The little girl nodded, then tugged on her father's coat. Alessandro bent down, and she whispered something in his ear.

Straightening, he grasped his daughter's hand. "Excuse us. We need to find the little girls' room."

"Are you all going to stay out here or come in and join the rest of us?" Lidia Vance asked from the entryway of the living room.

Max smiled at his wife. "We're coming." Waving everyone into the room, he took up the rear. "She takes her role as hostess very seriously."

The petite Italian woman, elegantly attired in a cream-colored dress that complemented her olive skin and dark eyes, looked pointedly at her husband. "One of us has to."

Inside the room Michael, accompanied by Layla, came up to Becca. "I think I'm the only one in the family who hasn't said thank you, Becca."

"Okay, but if you all keep doing that, I'm gonna get a swelled head. It was my job to find the person responsible for all these murders."

Michael combed his fingers through his thick brown hair. "Do you think Escalante had something to do with the disappearance of my two foremen?"

"With all that's happened, yes. Dahlia's diary mentioned that it had been necessary for both of your foremen to be taken out of the picture. Those were her words."

Anger descended over Michael's features. "I kept hoping that wasn't the case. I feel responsible. If they weren't working for me, maybe—"

Layla rubbed her hand up and down his arm. "Michael, you didn't know about Escalante. No one knew he was alive for months. Who would have thought he would do what he did?"

"Revenge is a powerful emotion." Michael shook his head.

"I have to agree, and Escalante had a lot of revenge in him," Quinn said.

Becca caught sight of the diamond ring on Layla's left finger. "I haven't had a chance to congratulate you two on your engagement. When's the big day?"

"We've been discussing it. Colleen's wedding is making me realize I don't want to wait too long." Michael peered down at Layla, love in his expression.

Becca's heart skipped a beat. She wanted Quinn to look at her like that. Instead he was distant. Not cold, but not his usual warm self. They needed to talk. She wasn't ready to walk away.

"And now that things will be returning to normal, we can have discussions on exactly when we'll get married," Layla said, flipping her long hair behind her shoulder, her beautiful silver bracelets sparkling in the light.

Yes, normal. Becca didn't feel her life was normal at the moment. Even with the end to the rash of murders and their investigations, everything around her was torn apart like her kitchen had been.

Frank Montgomery stood at one of the tables set up for dinner and raised his sparkling cider for a toast. "I haven't seen my daughter this happy—ever. To you, Alessandro, for bringing that smile to her. You are welcomed with open arms into the Montgomery family."

His uncle's salute surprised Quinn. A powerfully built man, stocky and muscular, he rarely expressed his sentiments. His words spurred his own desires for a family, to have a woman welcomed into the Montgomery fold. He slanted a look toward Becca seated next to him. He'd thought for a brief time she might be that woman. But how could she be, when every time she left for work he would worry? One day the worry would become too much, eroding their relationship. He wouldn't do that to Becca or himself.

Quinn lifted his glass and touched Becca's to his right, then Pastor Gabriel's eight-year-old daughter,

Hannah Carter's, to his left. Then he made his own toast. "To family. May you two have many babies." He knew his cousin wanted children as much as he did.

Hannah giggled, the pink beads in her hair bouncing. "Mr. Quinn, you're sweet."

"Not half as sweet as you are, Miss Hannah."

"I'm Sarah." She giggled some more, covering her mouth with her hand.

"I know your mother's trick. Pink beads for Hannah and purple for Sarah. You have to wake up pretty early to fool me."

The little girl's dark eyes sparkled with mischief. "We traded."

Quinn looked toward Susan Dawson, the twins' mother.

She shook her head. "She's pulling your leg, Quinn. That's Hannah. I caught them and made them change back before coming."

Becca followed the exchange that Quinn carried on with Hannah for the next few minutes and her throat constricted. Everywhere she turned she was struck with the fact Quinn was great with children and wanted a house full of them. When she pictured her future, she didn't see kids in it. She'd been mother and father to Caitlin and Todd for so long, she wanted to know who Becca Hilliard was without children around. She had just begun to get a sense of that woman.

Becca averted her gaze from Quinn. It hurt too much to look at him and see what would never be. She shifted her attention to Reverend Gabriel Dawson, who was sitting on the other side of her at the table. She'd found her father's Bible and had started reading it again this past week. It had sparked memories of the times she had spent with her father listening to him read a part of it to her, his arm around her. Feelings of security and peace had enveloped her. She wanted that back.

"Pastor Gabriel, I'd like to meet with you next week. Is that possible?"

"Is there a problem?" the minister of the Good Shepherd Christian Church asked, his eyes kind.

"It's been a while—well, years since I've attended church regularly. I've been wrestling with why I left in the first place."

"Say no more, Becca. I'll be glad to help you. I'm available tomorrow morning."

"But what about the wedding?"

"It's not until two. I see no reason to put off the discussion until sometime next week. Why don't you come to my office at nine?"

"Fine. I'd heard rumors you were a former Marine, and I believe they're true. You're definitely a take-charge man."

"Yes, to both."

"Did I hear the word 'rumor'?" Quinn asked, taking the last bite of his Italian cheesecake. "Are you two discussing my mother?"

"Never," Pastor Gabriel said, his gaze twinkling. "Your mother is a treasure who keeps me informed of what's going on."

"Such a nice way to put it." Quinn tipped back his glass and finished his cider.

The reverend responded to his teasing with, "She's involved in so many things at the church that I'm not sure how it would function without her."

"The operative word is involved. My mother never does anything halfway."

"Ah, that definitely describes Fiona," Sam interjected. "Did you know that she talked Mercedes Cortez into running a nursery at the church tomorrow during the wedding so that the children could attend the reception? She told my mother that this was a family affair and the kids need to be there to enjoying the celebration."

"Michael's housekeeper's daughter?" Quinn asked.

"Mercedes is an elementary-school teacher. She said she would gladly do it. Now I don't have to worry about Dario and Isabella during the wedding ceremony." Jessica passed a napkin to her older daughter to wipe her face.

"By herself?" Becca scanned all the tables filled with adults and many children.

"She has a friend who is going to help. Besides, it's only the youngest ones," Jessica answered.

"Yeah, Sarah and Hannah wouldn't miss this wedding. It's all they've been talking about for days."

"I'm the flower girl," Jessica's five-year-old daughter, Amy, piped in. "I get to throw flowers."

"Rose petals, honey." Sam took his napkin and cleaned off the smear on Amy's face that she hadn't touched when wiping it.

Becca relaxed back in her chair, sated with a delicious meal of shrimp and steak, listening to the conversation flowing around her at the table. The children were right there in the middle of the whole exchange, offering their opinions and comments. The warmth that settled in the pit of her stomach spread outward. She missed this with her siblings.

As Quinn escorted Becca to her front porch, a light illuminating it in softness, she thought of the long, silent ride from Colleen's rehearsal dinner. Several times she had tried to start a conversation and couldn't with Quinn's one-word answers. She'd given up.

In her usual tactic of confronting a problem head-on, Becca turned on the top step and said, "Please come in. I think we need to talk."

Quinn paused several stairs below her, his face concealed by the night. "I agree. But let's talk out here on the porch."

What was he afraid of? That she'd become hysterical and cause a scene if they were inside where it was more private?

As if he'd read her mind, he added, "It's a beautiful night."

She sank onto the love seat with enough room for Quinn to sit next to her. He remained standing, leaning back against the railing near her, his hands gripping the wood, his legs crossed at the ankles. In that moment he looked like a rich millionaire in a whole different league than she. That and the fact he didn't take a seat next to her spoke loud and clear the end of the evening wouldn't go well.

"Talk to me about my shooting. Ever since it happened, you've been pulling away." As she spoke, her heart slowed to a throbbing ache, as though she knew what he would say and was preparing herself.

"I brought Escalante into your life."

"What? I'm a homicide detective. Escalante killed people in my town. He brought himself into my life."

"I think he targeted you at the siege because he knew we were dating."

"That's possible, but he's dead. He won't be targeting me any longer."

Quinn dropped his head, his gaze boring into the floor. "Maggie and I argued right before she was called to defuse the bomb that killed her. I'm responsible for her not being as careful as she normally was."

His words, spoken so quietly, electrified the air between them, snatching Becca's response.

"I can't bear any more responsibility."

She wanted to take him into her embrace and remove the guilt that riddled him. She couldn't. Only he could. "What did you two argue about?"

"Her job. I wanted her to resign from the bomb squad. She wasn't ready. She enjoyed the challenge. Wanted to do it for at least a few more years."

"Do you trust God?"

Quinn's eyes widened, then he blinked several times. "Of course. What's that got to do with this?"

"Then put your trust in God to know what's best. Isn't that what you've been telling me?"

"Yes, but—"

"There are no buts. What should work for me should work for you, too."

Shaking his head, he pushed himself off the railing, nothing nonchalant about his stance. "It's not that simple."

"Oh, so there are two different standards for us?"

"No," he said harshly.

"I know emotions aren't simple and that's what we're talking about here. I think we should back off from each other. I am who I am. Being a police officer is part of me. That isn't going to change in the near future." She rose from the love seat, weariness clinging to her like sweat in a hundred percent humidity. "But Quinn, you might talk to someone about your guilt over Maggie's death. Things will happen that you won't have control over. Maggie's accident was one of those incidents."

"I know I can't control everything." Anger edged his voice.

Spent, she couldn't afford to invest any more emotion in this relationship. It hurt already so much to think she wouldn't see him again. But what would happen if they continued and these problems couldn't be resolved? "Besides my job, you and I don't see eye to eye on having a family."

"And there are our religious beliefs."

"Yes," she murmured, even though she wasn't sure that was as much an issue as before. "So I think we should go to the wedding tomorrow separately."

"Cut our losses?" The steel thread continued to run through his words.

"Yes."

"I agree." He strode toward the steps.

For a few seconds Becca wanted to go after him and

beg him to try and work out their differences. All couples had them. But then she remembered her own fear when Quinn was Escalante's target and realized she was as guilty as Quinn for worrying about losing a loved one. Her father's death had thrown her life into turmoil and was still, after all these years, ruling how she approached relationships. Stunned by that realization, she watched Quinn pull out of her driveway and drive away from her for the last time.

The heaviness in her chest seemed to explode outward, causing her to grasp the column next to the steps to steady herself. The ache in her shoulder from the sudden movement only reinforced her conviction that if she felt this bad *now,* she could imagine how awful it would be after investing more time in their relationship.

Yep, much better to cut her losses now rather than later, she thought, shoving herself away from the column and heading to her front door.

Quinn drove a block away from Becca's without really seeing the street before him. Pulling over to the curb, he turned off his truck before he had an accident. Gripping the steering wheel, he stared out the windshield, again not really seeing what was before him. All he could focus on was the terrible ache in his chest that was spreading.

You might talk to someone about your guilt over Maggie's death.

Becca's words haunted him. He hadn't told another soul about what had happened right before Maggie's death. Why Becca? Why now?

Lord, I'm lost. What do I do?

Talk to someone. The advice lingered in his thoughts. The impulse to turn his truck around and go back to Becca's and talk to her about it made his hands tremble. He grasped the steering wheel even tighter.

No, he couldn't. She had ended it with him.

Then who?

A name came to mind, and Quinn quickly started the engine. Twenty minutes later he rode the elevator up to his younger brother's high-rise apartment, praying he was home from the rehearsal dinner. Brendan, Chloe and her children had left earlier than he and Becca. When Quinn rang the bell, he breathed a sigh of relief when he immediately heard the door being unlocked.

Surprise flitted across Brendan's features. "What brings you here so late?" He studied Quinn's face. "What's wrong? Mom? Dad?"

Pushing past his brother, Quinn entered and made his way to a brown leather couch, collapsing onto it. "Mom and Dad are fine. It's over between Becca and me."

Brendan's green gaze honed in on Quinn. "What happened?"

"Ever since she was shot, I've been pulling back from her. I tried not to, but all I could think about was Maggie dying on the job and then Becca coming so close to doing the same. An inch or two lower and she would have died."

"But she didn't."

Quinn plunged both hands through his hair. "What about next time? This past week I haven't been able to sleep, thinking about all the possibilities."

"What about them? Do you worry about me every time I go on the job?"

Quinn shook his head. "It's not the same thing."

"Are you using what happened to Maggie to keep a woman at arm's length?" Brendan sat in a chair, leaning forward. "Are you afraid to put your heart on the line again?"

Quinn surged to his feet, his arms stiff at his sides. "I want to get married. I want a family."

"Whoa, there." Brendan held up his palms. "You're saying one thing and meaning something else." He came to his feet and met Quinn's gaze. "Death is part of life. We don't get to choose when it happens. All we can do is live the best life possible with the time given us. If you keep throwing roadblocks up between you and a woman, you won't get married and have that family you want so much."

"But—"

"I know you love me and care what happens to me, so ask yourself why you don't spend sleepless nights fretting about *my* hide and yet you do worry about Becca. You haven't known her a long time. So what makes her so special?"

I care—too much, Quinn thought, striding toward the door.

"Quinn?"

He glanced back at Brendan. "Yeah?"

"When did you stop putting your trust in the Lord?"

ELEVEN

"Becca, you ask some good questions. There's nothing wrong with questioning the Lord. But in your questioning, you need to search for answers, too. Our faith grows that way." Pastor Gabriel sat in a chair across from Becca in his office at the church.

"I've lost touch with the Bible. Do you have any Bible study classes?"

"We're actually starting a new one in a few weeks. You're welcome to join it. We'll be examining the four Gospels. It'll meet on Sunday afternoons."

She uncrossed her legs and rose. "That sounds perfect. I don't usually work on Sundays, so I should be able to make most of the classes."

Pastor Gabriel came to his feet. "I'm glad you've decided to join us. I'm here to answer any of your questions."

"I appreciate it." Becca shook his hand, then left his office.

Out in the hall she paused, splaying her palm over her heart. She felt lighter, freer. This felt so right, as though she had come home when she had entered the church this morning and met with Pastor Gabriel. She'd been up most the night wavering between her intense, painful emotions tied up with Quinn and this budding excitement that she had returned to the fold and only good things were in store for her spiritually.

Lord, I need help with the rest of my life.

Now if she could just forget Quinn and get the rest of her life in order. She realized she was committing herself to seeing him every week at church, but Pastor Gabriel was an inspiration. She would have to make sure to attend the service Quinn didn't, at least until her emotions were locked away so tightly that the sight of him wouldn't affect her. Right? When would that be?

A year? Ten?

The hardest thing she'd done was tell him she couldn't see him anymore. She didn't see how it would work between them. If he couldn't accept her for who she was, then it wasn't going to work.

A commotion in the foyer drew her attention. She walked down the corridor and spied Jessica with Amy and Isabella. "What are you all doing here?"

Jessica whirled around, surprise widening her eyes. "I could ask you the same question. Staking out your seat for the wedding early?"

"Ha! No, I was even considering not coming."

"Becca, you hafta come." Amy padded over to her, staring up at her. "Please. I want you to see me. I've got a new dress."

Becca knelt in front of the little girl. "You're going to be the prettiest flower girl there is."

"I can be yours. I'll know what to do. Mommy and me are gonna practice now so—" Amy glanced back at Jessica "—so I don't make a mistake."

"You'll be great. If I ever get married, you can be my flower girl," Becca said around the lump that lodged in her throat. The chances of that happening anytime in the near future were slim to none.

"Will you come? You can sit with us." Amy tapped the toe of her black patent-leather shoe on the tile floor. "I'm breakin' these."

Becca chuckled and straightened. "I'll be here for your big debut."

Amy scrunched up her brow. "De—boo?"

"Grand entrance."

The child's expression brightened.

"I think that's a great suggestion, Amy. Becca, why don't you come with us? With all that's happening I could use an extra pair of hands, especially with Sam and Amy participating in the wedding party."

"Aren't you going to leave the twins in the nursery during the ceremony?"

"Yes, but that's only for an hour or so."

"I think I've just been conned into babysitting."

Jessica tsked. "Now, what are good friends for? To help out in emergencies."

"And this is an emergency? You'll have tons of family around to help."

"I know, but you're like family to Sam and me."

"You don't have to say another word. I'd love to help you with your children. You know I adore them."

"You should have some of your own."

"Jessica, don't go there," Becca said with a mock warning because this was a subject that Jessica had brought up on more than one occasion, especially after she'd had the twins. She thought everyone should be a mother.

"Will you do me another favor?" Jessica jiggled Isabella from one arm to the other. "Will you hold her while I walk Amy through what she's going to do?"

"Sure. Where's Dario?"

"He's at home with Sam."

Jessica passed the baby to Becca, then took her eldest daughter's hand and led her into the sanctuary. Becca followed behind the pair, rocking Isabella up and down in her arms. Isabella laughed and fingered Becca's face. Her distinctive baby-powder scent prodded memories of holding her siblings when they were little. She could remember cradling Caitlin to her and telling her she would protect her forever, that she would always love her. That overpowering feeling of completeness engulfed her again while holding Isabella. It stunned her and left her shaken.

She'd held babies before, but never with this sensation that, like walking into the church, she had come home. If Jessica hadn't been busy parading Amy down the center aisle, she would have thrust the baby back into her mother's arms and fled. Had Quinn done this to her? Had he sparked a latent desire to be a mother? She'd been one—well, a surrogate one for her sister and brother. She didn't want her own kids. Did she?

Yes, she'd relished raising her siblings. The school functions, the ball games, the homework, the weekend camping trips, the picnics in the mountains. They had shown her the positive side to life when often all she saw as a police officer was the negative.

Could she be a mother—carrying her own baby inside her for nine months and giving birth? She shook the question from her mind and centered her full attention on what Jessica and Amy were doing. The second she gave Isabella back, the feeling would be gone and she would be back on track—finishing her degree, working, building her life without children. If she needed a baby fix, she could always turn to one of her friends and hold theirs.

"Thanks, Becca." Jessica in front of her with her arms open.

Becca blinked and quickly relinquished Isabella to her mother. But when her arms were empty, she felt empty. She pushed the feeling down. Breaking up with Quinn was causing her to be extra emotional. Once she was back in her regular routine everything would return to normal.

Becca moved away. "I need to leave if I'm going to be back here in time for the wedding." She glanced around the church already set up with beautiful orchids.

Had she lost her chance at something like this? She was afraid that after knowing Quinn, no one would live up to him. Tears threatened. She spun on her heel and fled the sanctuary before Jessica asked her why her eyes glistened.

Becca carried Isabella while Jessica held Dario, both of them making their way toward the nursery. Sam had

Amy in tow. At least, sort of, Becca thought with a smile. The little girl danced around in her pale-pink dress with glitter and stars in her hair.

Near the door to the nursery a woman with straight black hair and large dark-brown eyes greeted the children as they came in. She offered Jessica and Becca a smile and took Dario from Jessica.

"He's adorable. I'm Mercedes Cortez and your children will be in good hands. Don't worry." She placed Jessica's son on the floor in front of a big stuffed bear he immediately grabbed.

"That's Dario and this is his twin sister, Isabella," Jessica said while Becca settled Isabella next to her brother. "I want to thank you for doing this."

"I owe Michael Vance for being so good to my parents. He's the best employer. Besides, I love kids. And my assistant is Donita at school."

Becca stepped away from Jessica and Mercedes and surveyed the children already in the large nursery. Manuel walked around carrying a truck. Elijah Dawson, the reverend's son, held a bottle filled with juice. Sofia Vance, Sam's niece, slept in the crib and Sean Montgomery, Adam's son, sat in a high chair eating pieces of a banana. Another couple Becca recognized as Dr. Robert Fletcher and his wife, Pamela, brought in their toddler.

The nursery would be full before too long. Seeing all the children surrounding her made her arms ache. Becca had the sudden urge to scoop Isabella back up into her embrace and hug her to her chest, never letting the baby go. She didn't understand it, but she couldn't shake the empty feeling boring into her as she walked away from the room with Jessica.

Boy, did she need to get back to work. She'd been off for ten days and the inactivity had driven her crazy. That could be the only explanation, she decided as she emerged into the large church foyer where people were waiting to sign the guest book. Susan Dawson and Emily Vance manned the table where the book was, welcoming the guests as they penned their names.

Jessica and Becca fell into line. Soft organ music drifted from the sanctuary. Love songs, Becca noted wistfully. Out of the corner of her eye she caught sight of Quinn approaching his mother. With him dressed in a tuxedo again, his appearance brought to mind the scene on the porch the night before. He said something to Fiona, started to turn away, paused and twisted around to stare at her across the foyer.

The sensation of time coming to a standstill inundated her and the rest of the people faded from her consciousness. All she saw was Quinn, appearing incredibly handsome with a pinched look about his mouth and a tiredness in his gaze. From lack of sleep—like her? When she'd told him it was probably for the best that they didn't see each other, he hadn't protested. He had accepted what she had said and left her to ache silently at her loss.

His mother saying something to Quinn jerked his attention away. Becca used that moment to murmur to Jessica, "I'm going on in and getting us a seat. I'll sign the book later."

"Get a seat close to the front. I need to be near if Amy needs me."

Becca had almost made it to the doors into the sanctuary when a hand on her shoulder stopped her. She didn't need to see who it belonged to. She knew Quinn's touch. She wasn't sure she would ever forget it.

"You look beautiful, Becca."

His soft words washed over her in waves of yearning. His familiar aftershave swamped her, robbing her of any response.

"We may not be dating anymore, but can't we at least be friends?"

No! She knew she couldn't take being around him and not want to be with him.

"I mean…"

She glanced back at the troubled expression on his face. Her heart lurched.

"I don't know what I mean. I guess it's silly to think we can be friends. Although you and Sam dated and you're still good friends." He rubbed his hand along the back of his neck. "Forget I said anything."

It had been different with Sam. She hadn't fallen in love with him as she had with Quinn. That realization heightened the pain.

"I see you're with Jessica."

"Yes," she said, finally finding her voice through the ache that encompassed her. "She needed help with the twins since Sam's with the wedding party."

Any previous awkwardness melted as he said, "I saw you walking in with Isabella. You're a natural."

Don't remind me! Her maternal instincts were leaking out of the box she'd locked them in. "I've had practice." She needed to end their conversation before she threw herself into his embrace and didn't care that they disagreed on some major issues. "I'd better get inside. The wedding is going to start soon."

Quinn peered at his watch, one corner of his mouth hitching up. "Yeah, in another twenty minutes."

"Jessica wants a good spot up front."

"There's a section roped off for the families."

Okay, I need to escape you. Is that what you want to hear? "See you at the reception," she said in parting, realizing she'd have to make a point to stay away from him afterward.

Her composure was too fragile right now to subject herself to a constant dose of Quinn Montgomery. Maybe in a year…or ten. Becca hurried inside the sanctuary, almost flying by the ushers.

Brendan stepped in front to stop her flight. "May I show you to a seat?" he asked, a smug smile on his face as though he had witnessed her talking with his brother and knew something she didn't. "Bride's or groom's side?"

"How about both? Okay, I guess I have to make a decision. Groom's side. Jessica and I are sitting together." At that moment she was so tired of making decisions, of being the strong one.

As she walked down the aisle with her arm through Brendan's, she thought back to the past week when Quinn would do something for her because she was recuperating. Every evening he'd had something for her to eat. He didn't join her, but the food was always there so she didn't have to worry about fixing something in her kitchen that wasn't quite put together or having to go out. It had been nice to have someone looking after her even if it was from afar.

Before she slid into the pew, Brendan whispered, "I noticed there was some tension between you and Quinn."

He didn't ask a question but his expression and tone indicated he was available to listen to her problems if she so chose. "Your powers of observation haven't diminished since you went to work for the FBI."

"He's my brother, but you and I are friends. I'm here if you need me."

She attempted a smile that faltered. "Thanks. I know. There really isn't anything to talk about. He's finished with my house and is moving on to other...projects."

Both of Brendan's eyebrows rose. "So this recent chumminess was due to the renovation he was doing?"

"You know how it is when you're forced into close quarters with another."

Brendan's chuckles peppered the air, rivaling the background organ music. "Yeah, thankfully. Otherwise Chloe and I might not be engaged." He glanced around at the pews beginning to fill up with guests. "Better get back to my job as an usher. I'll talk with you at the reception. I want to tell you about a visit from my brother last night."

With that parting, mysterious remark, Brendan sauntered away, leaving Becca ready to throttle him. What was that supposed to mean? He knew her curiosity would leave her mulling over his statement, trying to figure out what he had meant by it. Sinking down onto the pew, she clenched her jaw, hating the fact that for a few seconds hope had flared in her heart.

Then she remembered she had walked away from Quinn, that she had ended it because she had known it wouldn't have been long before Quinn did. She had just been the first to voice what they both had been feeling.

Jessica slipped in beside her. "They're almost ready to start."

"Where have you been?"

"Checking on the twins and Amy."

Becca laughed. "You've got it bad."

"What?"

"Being a mother."

"Nothing's wrong with that." Jessica lifted her chin, her chest expanding with a deep breath.

"I know," Becca murmured as the music changed, signaling the the beginning of the ceremony to the guests.

As she angled around to watch the procession, Becca fought the yearning for a child that was poking its head out again. Had she overreacted when Caitlin had left home, declaring to everyone she was through being a parent? Was she just being stubborn sticking by that declaration? Those questions flitted through her mind as Colleen, on the arm of her father, Frank, walked down the aisle toward Alessandro. The satin and lace gown with long train accentuated Colleen's curves while the veil did nothing to conceal the look of contentment on her face.

Becca was thrilled for Colleen and Alessandro. They deserved some happiness after all that had happened the past few months. But seeing the couple staring into each other eyes with such love ripped her own heart into shreds. She wanted a man to look at her like that. For a fleeting time she had thought that might be possible with Quinn until reality had set in.

Halfway through the ceremony Amy began dancing about. Nothing Holly or Chloe, who were the nearest bridesmaids, did stopped the little girl.

Jessica groaned. "She needs to go to the restroom." She started to rise.

Becca stopped her. "Let me. This is your family. Enjoy the rest of the wedding."

"I don't mind."

"Please."

There was probably a pained look in her eyes, Becca decided because Jessica relinquished her mommy role. Becca moved toward the side aisle where she would be less obvious and came around behind Amy. Taking the child's hand, she hurried to the side of the church and toward the back double doors.

Out in the foyer Amy whined, "Becca, I've got to go *bad.*"

"I know. C'mon."

Becca went toward the hallway that led to the classrooms and the nursery. Inside the restroom she waited for the little girl, then made sure Amy washed her hands when she was finished. When the little girl started to dry them on her dress, Becca pulled a paper towel out of the dispenser and gave it to the child.

"Mommy's always telling me not to use my clothes to dry my hands."

"Yeah, that's a mommy thing. Ready to go? We can sit at the very back."

Amy ran toward the door. Out in the hall she screwed up her face and turned toward Becca. "Why's that strange man coming out of the nursery?" she asked in a loud voice.

Hearing a child crying, Becca poked her head out, spying a dark haired man in the doorway into the nursery staring at Amy, his arm clutching Manuel, who wiggled, trying to get down, tears running down his chubby face.

Escalante!

He had come for his son.

In that moment the world came to a grinding halt. Then her police training kicked in. She pushed Amy behind her, saying, "Don't come out until someone you know comes and gets you. Promise?"

"Yes," came the shaky response.

Becca peered around the corner of the door frame and saw that Escalante had darted back into the nursery. She went for the gun that usually she wore at the small of her back. Of course, there wasn't anything there, and she'd left her purse with her weapon in it with Jessica in the sanctuary.

The screams coming from the nursery sent a chill down Becca. The slamming of its door alerted her to the hostage situation quickly developing with little children and two adults as the captives. Nothing could be worse, and she couldn't take back that she and Amy had been in the wrong place at the wrong time.

Becca went back into the restroom. "I've changed my mind. I need you to come with me. But you've got to stay behind me. Understand?"

The child's huge eyes widened even more, but she nodded.

With her body shielding Amy, Becca eased out into the hallway, her gaze glued to the closed nursery door. She backed down the corridor toward the sanctuary. She needed help.

At the entrance into the foyer Becca said, "Amy, I need you to get your daddy. No matter what he's doing, make him come here."

"What's wrong?"

Although she wasn't looking at the child because she had to keep her gaze trained on the nursery, Becca heard the tears in Amy's voice. She tried to maintain a calm tone when she replied, "I need your daddy's help. Now go."

The urgency prodded the little girl to race across the foyer and yank open the door into the sanctuary. Becca heard it swish closed, every fiber of her being vigilant for any movement from the nursery. She didn't even have her cell phone to inform the police, and she couldn't risk leaving to make the call.

Quinn kept looking toward the double doors that Becca and Amy had disappeared through. The second Becca left the sanctuary disappointment gripped him. He'd been able to sneak some glances toward her during the ceremony as he'd scanned the guests, allowing his gaze to linger a few seconds longer on Becca's beautiful face. Who was he kidding? How was he going to manage to walk away from her without being hurt? After the sleepless night before, he couldn't fool himself. He loved Becca Hilliard and didn't know how to bridge the gulf between their opposing sides on several key issues.

The sound of Pastor Gabriel's voice pronouncing Colleen and Alessandro husband and wife pulled him away from endless questions Quinn had asked himself for the past eighteen hours. A cheer rose from the crowd, followed by loud clapping. The Vances and Montgomerys were so ready to celebrate and this wedding was the perfect reason.

"Daddy, Daddy, Becca needs you," Amy screamed, running down the center aisle. She stumbled, fell but quickly scrambled to her feet and continued toward her father.

The fear in the child's eyes sent a shaft of his own fear straight through Quinn. He was in front of Amy a step ahead of Sam, kneeling down to the child's level while her father hovered over his shoulder.

"What's wrong with Becca?" Quinn asked, forcing himself to keep his voice steady and calm while all kinds of scenarios ran through his head—none of them good.

"There's a bad man in the nursery."

Those words struck terror in Quinn—and, he knew, in everyone else in the church. Sam stepped around Quinn and scooped his daughter up in his arms, deposited her into Jessica's, then strode toward the foyer with Quinn right behind.

At the back of the church as more people surged toward them, Quinn raised his hands and shouted over the din of concerned voices, "Please stay here until we assess the situation. I promise one of us will be back to let you all know what's going on." He quirked a reassuring grin that he couldn't maintain. "You know little kids' imaginations. Probably nothing to get alarmed about." He prayed to God he was speaking the truth, Quinn thought as he hurriedly followed Sam out into the foyer.

Quinn spotted Becca by the door that led to the classrooms and the nursery. By her rigid stance—alert, poised to move at a second's notice—he knew that Amy had described the situation quite adequately. A bad man was in there with the children!

"Becca, what's going on? Amy said—"

When Becca pivoted toward them, Quinn froze. The look, an almost panicked one until she got herself under control, confirmed Quinn's worst fears. Escalante hadn't died—again.

"Escalante tried to kidnap Manuel. He's holed up in the nursery with all the children. The door's closed and he hasn't tried to leave." She swung her gaze back down the length of the hall.

"Have you heard anything coming from the nursery?" Sam asked before Quinn could say anything.

"Shouts and screams, nothing else."

All the color drained from Sam's face. "Did he have a gun?"

Becca thought for a few long seconds, trying to visualize the too-brief scene again in her mind. "I think so. It happened so fast, but I think I saw one stuck in his waistband."

Escalante with a gun among their children. Quinn's legs nearly gave out on him. He braced his arm against the wall. They couldn't dwell on that.

"Have you called the police?" Quinn asked, pushing his fear to the back because it wouldn't do him any good. It wouldn't get the children out safely.

"I don't have my cell and I didn't want to leave this spot."

With trembling hands, Sam flipped his phone open and called the police to report what had happened at the church. "There'll be here as soon as possible, but I don't want to wait. Escalante's crazy with revenge and hates all Vances and Montgomerys. Most of that nursery is filled with kids with those last names."

Lord, protect the children, Quinn prayed.

"Let me try to negotiate," Becca said.

Sam shook his head, his attention fixed on the nursery door. "It won't help. He has nothing to lose now. We've got to do something fast."

"You can't storm the nursery." Alarm rippled through Becca's expression before she managed to control it.

Sam clenched his hands as though he wanted to punch the wall. "There has to be something we can do."

Quinn felt the same frustration. Their options were few. They didn't have— Suddenly a possible solution presented itself. "I've got an idea." Both Sam and Becca's gazes riveted to him, and he continued, working out the logistics in his head. "Our company built this addition to the church. We built a door into a storage area in the back of the closet in the nursery. We can get into the storage area through the heating shaft, then into the closet. He won't be expecting us. Hopefully we can surprise Escalante before he hurts any of the kids."

"It has to work." Sam headed for the sanctuary. "I'll get a team together and let everyone know what's going on. We have a church full of trained officers. Becca, do your thing. Maybe it will distract Escalante long enough to get us into the room."

Left with Becca in the foyer, Quinn said, "There's a phone line into the nursery. He might pick up." He moved toward the first room, which was an office with a phone. "Extension two-eight-three." He turned to leave, intending to be in on the raid. People he loved were in that room and he knew the way into it.

"Leave it to Sam, Quinn." Becca picked up the receiver.

"No. Aren't you the one who told me to trust in the Lord, that risks are part of life?"

"Yes, but I meant—" Becca didn't finish her sentence. Quinn was gone. She heard his footsteps on the tile floor, striding away from her.

She squeezed her eyes closed. *Protect them, God.*

Taking a deep, composing breath, Becca punched in the numbers, her hand clutching the tan receiver as though it were a lifeline. And perhaps it was for those children. A pounding behind her eyes vied with the ringing of the phone—insistent, annoying, never ending. Escalante wasn't going to pick up.

God, I need Your help.

That composing breath she had taken in seemed to spread throughout her body, relaxing her, directing her on the task at hand. God was with her as if He stood right next to her. Instinctively she shifted, staring at the empty space next to her, and felt comfort in the sense He was surrounding her with His love and power.

Suddenly the ringing stopped and a gruff voice said, "I will start killing children if I don't get safe passage to the airport, where a plane will be waiting to take me and my son out of the country."

The sound of crying in the background, of children wailing for their mommies, wrenched Becca's heart, but she couldn't allow that to distract her. "This is Becca Hilliard. That will take some time to arrange."

"I have nothing to lose now. If I am going down, so are a lot of Vances and Montgomerys. I will blow this whole place. There is one door into this room and I have it wired. Do not call back unless you have news for me. You have ten minutes before I start shooting."

"I can't—"

The phone slammed down, the noise vibrating down her length. Did Escalante have a bomb, too? From the frantic tone to his voice he sounded as though he had gone over the edge. How could he be alive? She'd seen— She didn't have the time to think about that.

Heading out of the office, she ran into the mayor. "We need to get everyone out of the church. Escalante has wired the nursery door and if anyone goes in through it, he'll blow the place up. He's given us ten minutes."

"Ten minutes! You think he would kill himself to spite us?" Max asked, his face looking as deathly pale as when he'd been lying unconscious in his hospital bed.

"Yes."

TWELVE

In the church foyer Quinn shed his tuxedo coat while Sam gathered the team going into the nursery, filling them on what they needed to do. Brendan and Alessandro took their jackets off, too, and checked the weapons they were going to use.

His younger brother thrust a gun into Quinn's hand. "You know how to use this. You may need it."

The heavy metal in his grip felt alien. He used to practice with Brendan at the shooting range and had done well, even better than his younger brother, but he had never shot at a live target. But if he had to, he would. Escalante's reign of terror would end *today*.

"Jake, will you coordinate with the police when they arrive? They should be here soon." Sam started toward the maintenance closet.

Max hastened toward them. "Son, Becca just told me that Escalante said the door into the nursery is wired, and he said he will start shooting—" the mayor glanced at his watch "—in nine minutes."

Sam blanched.

Quinn's stomach knotted. A bomb! Memories of the explosion at the hospital, of Maggie's death, flashed into his mind, making him go ice cold.

"I can disarm it once we get into the nursery," Alessandro said from behind Sam.

"What if the closet door is wired, too?" Quinn asked the question each of the men was thinking.

"No, I don't think it is," Max said. "Escalante told Becca he wired the only door into the nursery. I don't think he bothered with the closet."

"Let's pray you're right. We don't have much time," Sam muttered and resumed his path to the entrance into the heating shaft in the ceiling.

Quinn accompanied Sam, with Alessandro and Brendan right behind them. *Lord, watch out for the children.*

Becca hung up with her commander on the negotiation team. They were five minutes away. According to Escalante's deadline, there were six minutes left. Not enough time. But in hopes of stalling, she made another call to extension 283. She heard the ringing of the phone coming from the earpiece and from the hallway in the direction of the nursery. An eerie sensation snaked up her spine.

Max returned and stood in the doorway, alternating watching her and the nursery door. "They know about the bomb."

The ringing ceased. Becca tensed.

"What do you have for me?" Escalante practically shouted into the receiver.

"A helicopter is on its way to take you to the airport,

where a plane is being gassed for you. But it will take fifteen minutes."

"I want a car *now* before a sniper has a chance to set up a kill shot. One of the guests. You drive. I'm no fool. Don't play me for one. Bring it to the back door, pull right up to it. You've got four minutes." Escalante severed their connection.

Becca looked toward Max. "He wants a car now. I'm to drive him to the airport."

"No, I will. His beef is with me, not you." Rage mottled his face red.

"You aren't an option." Becca covered the few steps to Max and held out her hand for the keys. "I need your car. Where is it?"

"First row, the black Lexus."

"Do you have your cell phone? I'll need to call him when I'm parked at the back door." Hers was still in her purse.

Max fished into his pocket and pulled out his cell and car keys and gave them to her. "Maybe Sam will take Escalante out before it comes to that."

Going out the door, Becca said, "Either way, I'll make the call in two minutes."

She rushed through the foyer and out the main entrance, spying Max's car in the first row. Hundreds of people crowded the parking lot at a safe distance from the church, all their gazes on the building. Becca saw a few familiar faces, but she had no time to stop and explain what she was doing. She wouldn't—couldn't—let Escalante kill one child, even if it meant putting her own life on the line.

Switching on the engine, Becca saw the clock on the dashboard. Two minutes until— Her sweaty hands slipped on the steering wheel as she turned the sedan toward the back door, the pounding inside her head matching the frantic beating of her heart.

Quinn dropped down from the heating shaft in the ceiling into the storage area behind the nursery closet. The space was small but thankfully there weren't many boxes in it. While Sam descended to the floor, holding the only flashlight they could find, Quinn crouched down in front of the half door into the closet. With breath held he inched it open. Only the darkness of the closet greeted him. He eased through the opening with Sam following right behind him.

In Quinn's mind he heard the ticking of the clock, counting down the minutes they had left until Escalante started shooting children or blowing up the room, killing himself and anyone else in the vicinity. Were the police here yet? What was Becca doing? Was she a safe distance away with the others?

When all four men crowded into the closet, the light from under the door illuminated the small area even more. Escalante's rants could be heard over several of the children's cries. A woman's voice pleaded for Escalante to let the children go and just hold her.

Sam pressed his ear to the door, his hand on the knob.

"The children are my ticket out of here, lady," Escalante said. "Or no one will leave alive."

From the sound of Escalante's voice, Quinn didn't

think he was near the short hallway where the closet and a bathroom were situated. If their luck held, they could sneak into the corridor undetected.

Sam turned the knob slowly and pushed open the door inch by inch. Over Sam's head Quinn saw that the hallway was empty. Sam, with his gun drawn, clambered out of the closet. Quinn came right behind him with Brendan and then Alessandro.

Removing his gun, Quinn flattened himself against the wall, clasping his weapon at his chest, his gaze fastened to the mirror on the nursery wall, set up at an angle that offered him a partial view of the room. But he didn't see Escalante.

"What's taking her so long?" Escalante shouted over the whimpers of the children. "She doesn't have much—"

The ringing of the phone by the door cut into Escalante's raving. Each man was against the wall, poised to move on Sam's signal. Escalante shifted into Quinn's sight.

The dark-haired man snatched up the phone. "You got a car?" A pause. "I don't want to see anyone. If I do—" Another pause. "Okay. I'm coming out with a few hostages."

Sam dropped to the floor and snuck a peek around the corner into the main room, the hallway hidden by the row of cribs nearby. He popped back, murder in his eyes.

The pounding of Quinn's heart thundered in his ears, nearly drowning out Escalante's next sentence. "I know I am dead without a few insurance policies." The cackle that followed that statement chilled Quinn to the marrow of his bones.

The slamming of the phone ended the conversation. It would be now or never.

Becca called the mayor, who was still in the office she had used. "Max, he's coming out with some of the children. Please make sure everyone is out of the way. If he sees anyone—"

"Got you." Max hung up.

Becca pocketed the cell, not knowing when she would need to use it again. It looked like it was going to be her, Escalante and several children heading to the airport.

As she waited, all she could feel was the thudding of her heart against her rib cage, as though it were ticking off the seconds until Escalante came out with his human shields. Sweat ran down into her eyes, stinging them.

"I want that kid and that one. You are coming with me to take care of the brats."

"I can only handle one of them," Mercedes said in a steady voice.

Quinn remembered meeting her once at Michael's ranch. He had admired her poise then and now.

"You're lying. You're carrying my son and that little girl. You don't have a choice. Pick them up now." There was a pause for several seconds while Mercedes did as he demanded. "That's better. I'll take this baby."

Footsteps approached the set of cribs. From the

mirror on the wall Quinn saw Escalante place his gun on the bed while he scooped up Sofia Vance, the sudden movement startling the baby, who began to cry. Escalante cursed.

Sam gave the signal to move. Quinn surged forward, totally fixated on tackling Escalante before he could retrieve his gun from the crib. Quinn had a score to settle. The man had hurt Becca.

The commotion pivoted Escalante with Sofia held out in front of him in both of his hands. His eyes widened. With a glance toward his gun, he started to twist back to get it. Adrenaline-driven, Quinn slammed into Escalante while Sam wrestled Sofia from the man's hold.

Quinn and Escalante rolled on the floor strewn with toys. Something poked into Quinn's back as he mowed over it. Pushing all pain from him, he concentrated on pinning down Escalante. The man's vise-hard grip on one wrist threatened to snap it. With all his strength, Quinn brought his other hand down on his tormentor's grasp, severing its lock about him. He heard something break. Shock flooded Escalante's expression. Quinn moved quickly and sat on the man's chest, his arms held plastered to his sides with Quinn's knees.

Then Quinn pummeled his fist into the man's face, again and again. In his mind's eye all he saw was Becca lying in the hospital bed, bandaged, in pain. Then the children's faces seeped into his thoughts with their cries for their mommies and daddies echoing through his brain. Escalante was *not* getting away this time to rise again to torment the people Quinn cared about.

A hand on his shoulder halted Quinn's next swing.

"Quinn, leave something for the rest of us," Sam said in a shaky, teasing voice. "It's over. You've got him."

Quinn stopped in midair, his hand still clenched so tightly that he began to feel an aching throb. He looked up and surveyed the nursery while a moan issued from Escalante's swollen mouth. The children were okay. Trembling, Mercedes and her friend were all right, although Mercedes's assistant sobbed in the rocking chair while holding Colin Fletcher to her chest.

"What about the door?" Quinn asked, not moving from his position even though Escalante struggled to get a decent breath. He didn't care. He didn't want the man to pull anything.

"Alessandro's checking it out," Brendan said, hugging Sean Montgomery to himself.

"I have handled it. Thankfully, it wasn't a complicated device." Alessandro straightened, turning the knob.

Quinn tensed.

Alessandro pushed the door open. Fresh air, not laced with sweat and baby smells, rushed into the room, heralding that the horror was over. The siege had ended well. Alessandro stepped out into the hall.

Max's voice boomed through the silence. "Is anyone hurt?"

"Only Escalante, but he'll survive to stand trial." Alessandro came back into the room.

"Let's get everyone out of here," Sam said, holding his gun on Escalante, who still lay on the floor, his face cut and bleeding. "I've got him covered, Quinn. You can get up."

Slowly Quinn pushed to his feet, hovering over the

man as though daring him to make a wrong move. His chest rose and fell rapidly as he dragged air into his lungs. He curled and uncurled his hands at his sides as the adrenaline flow ebbed.

"Are you okay?" Sam asked, pulling Quinn's attention from Escalante.

He nodded.

"Good. Then help get these kids to their parents. Jessica will be beside herself until she can hold the twins in her arms. Will you take care of them for me?"

He concentrated on Sam's words, shoving down the rage that had seized him when he had seen Escalante. "Consider it done."

Quinn lifted first Isabella, then Dario into his arms and hugged them, relishing their sweet scent. Sam's daughter explored his left ear while Dario squirmed, wanting to go to his father. "Your daddy is busy, but I bet your mommy will be glad to see you two."

Quinn walked out of the nursery, past Max in the corridor by the office where he was on the phone and into the foyer, needing to see Becca, needing to hold her after he turned over the twins to Jessica.

Sam's wife flew across the parking lot, ignoring the police barricade that had been hastily set up. An officer tried to stop her, and she shook him off. Tears streamed down her face as she approached Quinn and took her babies, burying her face against them.

"Where's Sam? Is he okay?"

"Yeah. He's holding Escalante." Quinn scanned the crowd, his gaze briefly touching on Amy cuddled against Lidia Vance, before moving on. "Where's Becca?"

Jessica pointed toward the back of the church. "She was waiting for Escalante at the back door in Max's car."

The rage he had managed to suppress surged to the foreground. "Why?"

"Because that's what he'd demanded or he was going to start killing the children."

"But—"

"Quinn, what would you have her do?" Jessica asked in a tight voice. "That's Becca. She thinks of others before herself."

Plowing his hand through his hair, Quinn started for the back of the church, saying, "I know. That's one of the reasons I love her."

"Quinn Montgomery, you can't say that and walk away," Jessica shouted after him, but he kept walking, needing to hold Becca and tell her somehow they would work things out. There was no way after what had happened—how close they had come to death—that he wasn't going to insist they try.

"Thanks, Max. I'm coming inside." Becca snapped the cell phone closed and climbed from the Lexus still parked at the back door.

Relief lightened her steps as she covered the short distance to the building and walked inside. The cool air-conditioned air washed over her, chilling the film of sweat blanketing her. She saw Brendan carrying two children from the nursery and hastened forward, needing to see for herself that everything was over.

Hoping to find Quinn and make sure he was all right.

* * *

All Escalante could think of was that his only living son was crying for his mommy, and they were taking him away from *him,* Manuel's rightful father. Anger, hot and burning, gripped him in its talon, blinding him to any dangers. He ignored the pulsating throb in his wrist and centered all his energy on one thing: escaping to find *his* son.

Manuel belonged to him!

The wail of the last child as Donita left the room drew Vance's glance toward the door. In that split second Escalante kicked out and up, striking his enemy in a vulnerable place. He doubled over and Escalante leaped to his feet, flinging himself at one member of the Vance family.

He wrenched the gun from Vance's hand, pistol-whipping him with it. Vance crumpled to the floor, his eyes fluttering closed. As Escalante gave him a kick, leveling the weapon at Vance's forehead, a faint sound behind him caused him to spin around to find Becca coming toward him. She froze when he raised the gun and pointed it at her chest.

"Well, well. We finally get to meet. I enjoyed our little chats on the phone. Do you have the car out back like I requested?"

"Yes." Becca's gaze fixed on Sam, lying unconscious or worse on the floor. Blood flowed from a head wound, saturating the brown carpet.

"Let us leave before anyone figures out what has happened. Your life will depend on them not knowing." Escalante motioned for Becca to leave first with him right behind her, the gun sticking into her back.

"You can't get away, Escalante. Where do you think you can go that the police won't find you?" *Please, God, let Sam be alive.*

"I have places I can hide. I've been hiding for the past six months."

"But we found you."

As he hurried her toward the exit, he jabbed the gun hard into her back to remind her she was only a bullet away from death. "Only because I wanted you to. I led you to my cabin when the time was right. I needed you all to think I was dead so I could get to Manuel. That's why I staged that explosion. With the cave system under the cabin, it was easy. All I had to do was to find a homeless man to be me."

Becca wanted to point out that his plan had ultimately failed, but the man had a weapon aimed at her and no one knew that he had escaped. The hall was unusually silent and empty.

She thrust open the back door, sunlight streaming into the building. She blinked at its brightness and nearly faltered in her step to the black Lexus.

She started to open the passenger door when Escalante said, "You're driving."

A few minutes after entering the church, Becca sat behind the wheel of the getaway car again. Thankfully this time it was only her and Escalante, no children involved. She could live with that.

He hunkered down low, keeping the gun leveled at her. "Drive out the back way. Stop for no one."

Quinn came around the side of the church and started to call out to Becca, who had emerged from the back door. His words died in his throat when he saw Escalante right behind her with a gun trained on her. He ducked back out of sight, torn between wanting to go for help and rushing in to rescue Becca, which he knew wasn't a good idea. Before he could make a decision, Becca started the car and peeled away from the building, using the back road.

Pivoting, Quinn ran toward Max and a police captain. "Escalante's got Becca and they've taken off in your car."

"What? I thought—" Max thundered.

Sam staggered out of the church, holding his head, blood coursing down his pale face. He fell to his knees. Jessica screamed and raced for her husband. Max, Quinn and the police captain followed.

"Escalante—he's got my gun. He's—gone."

"That man has more lives than a cat," Max muttered, stooping down next to his son. "He's got Becca in my car. They've left."

Sam looked up, pain and worry reflected in his expression. "It's my fault. I took my eye off—"

"Son, that won't do us any good." Max put his arm around Sam on one side while Jessica did on the other.

"What about the SWAT team? Did they try to stop him?"

"We never set up our perimeter because the problem had been contained," the police captain said.

"I'll take care of this," Max said, lifting his son to his feet as a paramedic brought a gurney toward them. "Don't worry about Becca. We'll get her back. And Escalante." After helping Sam to lie down, he turned to the captain and gave a description of his car and its license number. "It's got a GPS system in it we can use to track it."

Quinn listened as the mayor and the police captain coordinated the search for Becca. Knowing where she was and setting her free were two different things.

Lord, I need You now more than ever. Please watch over Becca and bring her home to me. I know You gave me something precious that I didn't know what to do with. I won't make that mistake again. My trust is in Your hands.

"Faster," Escalante shouted, waving the gun near Becca's face.

Her body shook with the vibration of the ruts in the dirt road. "If I go any faster, this car will fall apart."

"I won't let them win. Manuel won't be raised by the Vances. I will make him love me and forget those people." He spit out the words *those people* bitterly.

"It's over. Why don't you turn yourself over to the police before you end up dead in a shootout?" She hated to think what would happen to her in the middle of a standoff. She was in God's hands now and determinedly put that worry away.

"They have to find me first. I'm good at eluding the police. I've had a lot of practice over the years. Don't you think I thought about what I would do if something went wrong at the church?"

The constant jarring made her jaw ache, intensifying the pounding in her head. Escalante seemed to know the city streets better than she, especially the remote ones. In less than ten minutes he had navigated them to this isolated back road. Where were the police? Did they even know she was gone? Was Sam all right?

Once they arrived at his destination, Becca didn't think he would keep her alive. It was going to be left up to her to get away. *God, I need You. Help me.*

"What kind of life can you give your son, always running from the police, looking over your shoulder? That's no way to raise a child. He deserves more than that." Although her adrenaline pumped rampantly through her, Becca schooled her breathing to deep inhalations and her voice to an even, calm level.

"He's mine. My blood. He's not a Vance," Escalante screamed.

He was losing control, Becca thought, grasping onto that fact as maybe being her only chance to get away from him before he killed her.

Escalante motioned with the gun, saying, "Turn here."

As Becca braked quickly, an idea popped into her mind. She made a hard turn, sending the car into a skid toward a tree. Jerking the wheel at the last second, she braced herself for the impact. The Lexus crashed into the cottonwood on Escalante's side, the shock wave from the collision streaking up her length. The sound of metal crunching assailed her ears, vying for dominance over Escalante's screams of outrage.

As the airbags deployed, she twisted to wrestle the gun from Escalante, who had flung his arms out as though that action would protect him. He didn't have his seat belt on and his head struck the side window, bouncing off the glass and shattering it.

The airbag pummeled her chest, trapping her before she could get the gun.

"We have them. The car's stopped up ahead," Max said in the front seat as he listened to the dispatcher, tracking the Lexus.

"We're five minutes out."

Quinn heard the words, but all he could think of was Becca at the hands of Escalante and what he had done to her because she had been dating Quinn. He desperately needed to hold her and tell her he loved her. He didn't care what she did for a living. He'd rather be with her for a short time than never with her.

Lord, You brought Becca into my life, and all I could think about was that she was a police officer like Maggie. Because I hadn't really dealt with Maggie's death, I pushed Becca away. Please give me a chance to tell her what I really feel.

"I see the car," Brendan said.

From the backseat Quinn leaned forward to get a better look. What he saw chilled his blood. Smoke poured from the crumpled Lexus, the front passenger side smashed in like an accordion. Flames began to dance along the hood. Fear as Quinn had never known it shoved his heart into rapid pounding.

Her body battered and bruised, as if she had gone ten rounds with a heavyweight boxing champion, Becca tried to wiggle out from the material pressing her back.

Escalante's airbag held him pinned against the seat and window at an odd angle for a few seconds before the bag deflated. His eyes closed, his face cut from the glass, he remained motionless, sagging forward.

Thank You, God.

Her mind hazy, she tried to move, but her airbag stayed inflated. Feeling around for the release on her seat belt, she encountered the button to adjust the seat. She pushed. Nothing happened. She struggled to drag air into her lungs. Breathing shallowly, she continued to search for the release but a light-headedness attacked her, blurring her vision.

Vaguely, as blackness hovered at the edge of her consciousness, she thought she smelled smoke. She made one last attempt to free herself, but her oxygen-starved mind screamed for a decent breath.

Quinn pushed open the back door before his brother came to a full stop near the wrecked Lexus. Racing toward the sedan as other vehicles arrived at the scene, he yanked on the handle on the driver's side. Nothing.

Squinting through the hazy smoke that had seeped into the interior, Quinn spied Becca slumped against the seat, the still-inflated airbag holding her captive.

Lord! Help!

He attacked the door with all his strength, jerking on the handle. On the third pull it gave and crashed open, throwing him off balance. He charged forward, reaching in to unsnap Becca's seat belt.

The sound of a fire extinguisher blasted through the

din of voices. He was aware of the others swarming around the Lexus like ants after a choice piece of candy, but he wouldn't move away until he had pulled Becca to safety. Max and Brendan were on the other side working to get Escalante out. The fire was winning the battle with the extinguisher.

After finally releasing her seat belt, Quinn took Becca by the shoulders and dragged her out. Her eyes fluttered open, and she tried to smile. She moaned.

"We have to stop meeting like this," she choked out as she try to take deep breaths, then started coughing.

"Me taking care of you? Never!" He laid her on the ground, visually checking her out.

She shot him a confused look, wincing as her chest rose with each inhalation. "What do you mean?"

"Okay? Anything broken?"

"I don't think so. Just had the breath knocked out of me. Hurts to breathe."

He hoisted her up in his arms and hurried her away from the burning Lexus. Two men hauled an unconscious Escalante out of the car while the rest began to back off as the fire, fed by oxygen, ballooned into the air, black smoke roiling.

The explosion nearly toppled Quinn to the ground with Becca in his arms. He tightened his hold, steadied himself and kept moving. Another blast sounded, smoke and fire shooting up into the sky as though a rocket had been launched.

A safe distance away from the burning wreckage, Quinn collapsed to his knees with Becca still in his embrace and drew her as close as he could to him. "You are alive. Thank You, Lord."

* * *

"If you keep ending up here, the hospital will have to rename this room the Rebecca Hilliard Suite," Quinn said from the doorway, a large bouquet of lilies in his hand.

Her throat raw from the smoke inhalation, she choked out, "Funny." She pushed herself up. "I'm leaving this joint just as soon as the doctor comes by."

"I guess I don't have to ask if the breathing treatments worked."

She patted her chest. "As good as new. It takes more than a little smoke—" she coughed several times "—and a few bruises to get me down." Shifting to make herself more comfortable, she winced as a sharp pain knifed through her. "Well, maybe just as soon as my ribs heal."

Quinn took the chair next to her bed, placing the vase on the table beside Becca. "Escalante is under guard down the hall. Sam isn't taking any chances. I think half the police force is taking turns making sure Escalante doesn't escape while being treated."

"I'll feel a whole lot better when he is permanently behind bars."

Quinn grasped her hand and brought it toward him, kissing the back of it. "He isn't going anywhere. The D.A. has enough on him to lock him up and throw away the key."

"How are all the kids?" she asked, thinking about how she would have felt if she had been one of the parents waiting for the outcome of the siege. As she had negotiated with Escalante for the children's release, she'd realized she wanted a child. Maybe not in the near future, but she wanted to experience what Holly and the others had gone through—carrying a baby for nine months and then delivering him. But the only one she wanted to be the father of her child was Quinn, and she had pushed him away.

"Scared, but the parents are dealing with that. They're just thanking God none of the children were hurt. Most of the kids didn't realize exactly what was happening."

"And Manuel?"

"Happy in the arms of his mother and father. I don't think Peter and Emily will be letting him out of their sight anytime soon."

"I can understand that feeling." Not sure what else to talk about with Quinn, Becca slid her glance toward the flowers. "They're beautiful, but you shouldn't have. I'm fine. In fact, I hope to be back at work tomorrow as planned."

Quinn chuckled. "I expected you to say something like that. You can take a few days off."

"I've got a lot of paperwork to fill out in regards to the incident yesterday at the church."

"Sam's taking care of that. He knew you would say that and told me to tell you he didn't want to see you until at least Wednesday."

"He's my partner, not my supervisor. Besides, he has his own injury to worry about."

"Actually, that came from the captain. And Sam told me his head is too hard to break."

She would have released a huff, but the action of breathing deeply hurt. So instead, she sent Quinn a frown. "I think there's a conspiracy going on here. What am I suppose to do with myself? I nearly went stir-crazy last week recuperating from the gunshot wound," she said in a teasing voice, but she studied Quinn's reaction to her words. Her job was a barrier between them she didn't know how to scale, short of quitting the police force. Could she walk away from something she enjoyed and be happy in the long run? In the middle of all that had happened at the church, she'd felt she was doing something that counted—trying to save some people from going through what she had when her father died in a hostage situation. That was important to her.

He frowned. "You're really gonna be difficult about this resting, aren't you?"

"Yep."

"You could go shopping for a new dress for Colleen and Alessandro's delayed reception next Saturday. The one you wore yesterday is beyond repair."

"Oh, good. I wondered what they were going to do since their wedding was disrupted."

"They delayed their honeymoon trip to Italy and re-scheduled the reception. This time it really will be a celebration of the end of Escalante's reign of terror. There's no doubt where he is now." He cupped her hand between his, stroking its back while staring down at their physical connection.

Silence stretched between them until Becca couldn't take it any longer. "Quinn," she whispered a hair before he said her name.

"You go first," she offered, her mouth suddenly

parched, the feel of his fingers surrounding hers heady. How in the world did she ever think she could walk away from Quinn?

"Will you go with me to Colleen's reception next Saturday? I know you said we should go our separate ways. What can I do to change your mind?"

"Nothing," she managed to get out.

Her answer sent his stomach plummeting as though he'd fallen off a ledge. She wasn't going to budge. "Becca, I understand how important your job is to you," he said, determined to make her see they could have a relationship beyond friendship. "I was wrong to ask you to choose between me and your career. I know now what you do is part of who you are. How can I ask you to cut that out of your life? That would be like me never making a piece of furniture with my hands."

Pain flitting across her features, she struggled to sit straight up in bed, swinging her legs over the edge so she faced him. "What are you saying, Quinn?"

"I'm saying I love you. I want you to give me another chance. I don't care if you don't want a family. How can I ask another woman to be a mother to my children when you're the one I love?" One corner of his mouth quirked. "I do have a lot of nieces and nephews. That will have to satisfy me."

She averted her gaze for a long second, then reestablished eye contact with him, wonder in her expression. "Actually, having children might be negotiable."

"It is?" He wound his arms around her.

"I have to warn you, I'm a tough negotiator. I've taken classes to perfect my technique."

"So we should date and see where this relationship leads?" Hope flared in him.

"Yes. The other night, I was letting my fear rule my heart. I've always kept an emotional distance because of what happened to my father. His death threw my life into chaos, changing everything. I became the care-giver in the house, even before my mother died." She pressed her hand along the side of his face. "Now I know I wasn't fully living, experiencing everything I should. I need to see where these intense feelings for you will lead us. I don't want to walk away."

Quinn looked deep into her eyes. "Great. I'm think-ing we shouldn't wait until next Saturday to go out. Since you're gonna be going stir-crazy, how about going to dinner and a movie?"

"Better yet, let's inaugurate my brand-new kitch-en."

Taking her face in his hands, he whispered his lips across hers. "I like your suggestion better. I can bring a movie to watch after you and I fix dinner together."

"Together," she murmured. "That's a beautiful word."

"I agree." Quinn deepened the kiss, pouring all his love into it.

EPILOGUE

Wearing an emerald green silk cocktail dress, Becca stood by Quinn's side, surveying the vast ballroom at the Broadmoor Hotel where Lucia Vance and Rafael Wright's wedding reception was being held. Quinn reached out and took hold of her hand, then entered the crowd, full of Vances and Montgomerys.

"I think half the city is here," Becca whispered.

"I know all of my family is here."

"Sam has been beside himself this past week with his baby sister finally getting married. Good thing it's been quiet at the station."

"Too cold for people to be out committing crimes," Quinn said, slipping his hand to the small of her back as he guided her through a group of guests.

"Yeah, but we're in the middle of the holiday season. We usually see more crimes." Becca glanced toward one of the large windows. "It's snowing again."

"I love cold weather. Perfect time to snuggle up."

She peered back at Quinn. "In front of a roaring fire."

"Sold. Let's skip out—"

Laughing, Becca pressed her fingers over his mouth to still his words. "There's no way we can leave for at least an hour, Quinn Montgomery. Your mother would never forgive you or me. Besides, Ken and Julianna are saving us a place at their table."

"Okay. One hour. Then we leave."

He caught her gaze and silently transmitted his desire to be alone with her. For the past five months they had been an inseparable couple, spending all their spare time together. Becca wanted more. She knew that each time Quinn had to say goodbye and go to his own home. More and more she found herself imagining them as a family with a child—maybe even two. A girl and a boy.

"I see Ken waving to us." Quinn steered her around several tables covered in white linen cloths with bone-china, silver and crystal place settings, giving the cream and gold room an added fairy-tale look, perfect for a wedding reception.

"I was excited to hear from Julianna the other day when I came to your office that she and Ken are now officially engaged. She said they'll get married in the spring."

At the table Quinn pulled out a chair for Becca, leaning down to whisper in her ear, "Love is in the air."

Shivers flashed down her. His breath teased her neck right before he kissed it. She didn't blush often, but she felt the heat singe her cheeks as Ken and Julianna sat across from her, watching their exchange.

"Is there anything you want to tell us?" Ken asked, a twinkle in his eyes.

Quinn took a seat next to Becca. "Your cousin looked beautiful this evening walking down the aisle."

"Yeah, but—"

Julianna gave Ken a look that shut his mouth.

"Okay, what's going on here?" Becca asked, narrowing her gaze on Quinn.

Innocence bathed his features. "Nothing. We were discussing the wedding. That's what you do at one."

Something was up, Becca was sure, and Quinn knew how much she wasn't into surprises. When she got him alone she would interrogate him further. After all, she was a police detective and had those skills down. She'd know what plot Quinn, Ken and Julianna were concocting by the end of the evening.

Holly slipped into the chair next to Quinn. "Sorry I'm late. I had to feed Faith before I could come. I can't believe she's already a chowhound—she's only six weeks old! Probably going through a growth spurt. Although with Jake as her dad, I imagine she'll be doing a lot of that."

Holly's husband settled into the last chair at the table for six. "I predict many restless nights in store for this father when Faith grows up."

"You'll rise to the occasion. Aunt Marilyn would probably say that you deserve every moment of it after the things you pulled as a teenager."

"Look who's talking, cousin," Jake said with a laugh directed at Quinn. "Should I go into some of the scrapes you and Ken got into?" He swung his gaze to Becca. "Better not. Your date is a cop."

"And what do you call yourself?" Quinn asked.

"I work for the FBI."

"Bringing down criminals. The same as Becca." Quinn slipped his arm along the back of her chair.

The proud tone in Quinn's voice warmed her. It had taken some time for him to adjust to her job as a homicide detective and sometime hostage negotiator, but they had both prayed about it and put themselves in God's hands. Worry consumed your energy; faith energized you.

"Did you see Colleen, Alessandro and Mia earlier at the church? They just got in from Italy for the holidays and wedding." Holly scanned the ballroom. "They're over there talking to Liza and Frank. I can't believe how much Mia has grown since the summer. Kids grow up too fast."

Becca saw the glow in Holly's expression. Motherhood suited her. *Thank You, Lord, for giving her Faith. I know how hard her pregnancy was.* Maybe one day she would experience motherhood from nurturing the baby in the womb and giving birth to raising the child. As her thirty-first birthday and the end of her college degree neared, thoughts of having a child of her own had grown.

Listening to the others talk while feasting on the meal, Becca knew how lucky she was to have come home to the Lord and found a wonderful set of friends. Even though she wasn't a part of Quinn's family, they always made her feel as if she were.

Exactly an hour after she and Quinn had arrived at the reception, Quinn placed a hand on her arm and bent toward her. "Let's go. We've put in our appearance."

She wanted to be alone with him. Suddenly she needed to know where their relationship was going. Escalante's threat was gone now that he was going to prison for murder and drug trafficking. Even the last mystery surrounding Escalante had been solved when Michael had seen his picture in the paper. Escalante had been Hector Delgato, Michael's supposedly missing foreman, which certainly explained a lot about what had happened at Michael's ranch last spring.

The best thing that had happened over the past few months was that she and Quinn shared a deep faith and a love for each other. But she wanted more—her own family with him.

She pushed her chair back, said her goodbyes and threaded her way through the crowd to the exit with Quinn by her side. He helped her slip into her black wool coat and then held the door open for her. She stepped outside to the softly falling snow.

Looking up at it reflected in the lights from the hotel, she felt as if she had entered a dreamland. The blanket of white cushioned all sounds, making it quiet, and everything pure and clean. She took a deep breath of the crisp air, relishing the hint of burning wood. Someone had a fire going. That thought turned her to what Quinn and she had discussed earlier about going home to snuggle before a fire. She started for Quinn's truck.

He halted her. "What's the hurry?"

"I was thinking about that fire and snuggling."

"We don't need a fire to snuggle." He drew her into his embrace, pulling her up against him.

Snow continued to fall, her eyelashes catching a few

flakes. "That's true." She couldn't resist the impish grin that graced his expression. He was up to something. "Okay, what's up?"

"This." He knelt on the fallen snow, reached into his coat pocket and produced a small box. "Will you marry me, Rebecca Hilliard?"

The air swooshed from her lungs at the look of love that molded his expression, illuminated by the lamplight in the parking lot. He rose and tugged her to him.

"Speechless. That's most unusual."

She blinked, throwing her arms around him. "Yes. Yes! If you hadn't asked me soon, I would have asked you. Time's running out if we are going to have a family."

Joy gleamed in his eyes. "Then I think we should beat Julianna and Ken and have a Valentine's Day wedding."

She answered him by rising up on her tiptoes and planting a deep kiss on his mouth. She had come home.

* * * * *

Dear Reader,

In *Hearts on the Line,* both Quinn and Becca have to learn to trust in each other but mostly in God. Even Quinn, who has a strong faith in the Lord, doesn't put his trust in God totally. He is scared to put his heart on the line again and love Becca as she deserves. Trust is hard to give over to someone else. But that is what faith is all about—putting your trust in God that He knows best.

I hope you enjoyed Quinn and Becca's journey toward loving and trusting each other as well as God. Along the way, their faith and love are tested as they fight for their lives and the lives of their loved ones.

Also in this book, I had to delve into the life of a hostage negotiator. I was fortunate to interview a female hostage negotiator with a police department in my area. My respect and prayers go out to these men and women who have a very difficult job, trying to save lives in highly emotional situations. Captain Carole Newell coined the phrase "captive victim situation," which I use in my story in a domestic incident that turns into a barricade situation.

I love hearing from readers. You can contact me at P.O. Box 2074, Tulsa, OK 74101, or visit my Web site at www.margaretdaley.com where you can sign up for my quarterly newsletter.

Best wishes,

Margaret Daley

DISCUSSION QUESTIONS

1. Becca watched her mother die a slow, painful death, and as a result, turned away from God. Have you gone through something similar, where you questioned God and doubted your faith? How did you deal with it? What Scripture helped you get through it? "For by grace are you saved through faith; and that not of yourself: it is the gift of God." What does Ephesians 2:8 say about faith?

2. To Becca, control was important so she wouldn't experience the pain she did when both her parents died a few years apart. Do we have control of our lives? Why did Becca think control was the answer to her problems? What could have helped Becca?

3. Emotions got in the way for Becca on her job as a homicide detective. She had a hard time being as objective as she thought she should. Do you think police officers should keep their emotions locked up while on the job? How can a police officer be effective when he/she is continually bombarded by the evil in this world?

4. When Quinn created a beautiful piece of furniture, he felt closer to God, as if he was paying homage to the Lord as he carved the wood. Do you have something you do that makes you feel that way? How do you use your talent to glorify the Lord? How do you feel when you do it?

5. Quinn turned away from having a relationship with a woman because of the tragic death of his fiancée. Grief is a powerful emotion. How have you dealt with grief in your life? What has helped you the most while going through the grieving process?

6. Becca knew that Quinn wanted a family while she didn't, because she had already raised her siblings. How would you resolve this dilemma of two people who, although they care deeply for each other, are at polar opposite ends of a problem? How can your faith help you deal with this dilemma?

7. Becca's dream of finishing school and getting her psychology degree was important to her. Dreams are important to people. When do you cut your losses and give up on your dream? Should you give up your dream if it might hurt someone else if you don't?

8. Quinn had to learn that risk is part of life. When and how have you had to learn that? What risks are important enough to take? What risks should not be taken? Where do you draw the line?

9. Quinn was scared for Becca during the hostage situation. Have you ever had a situation that frightened you? Did your faith strengthen you and allow you to get through it? How? What Bible verses come to mind when thinking about fear and the Lord? "So that we may boldly say, the Lord is my helper, and I will not fear what man shall do unto me." What does Hebrews 13:6 say about fear?

10. In this book Becca went through a makeover for a date with Quinn. She never really cared that much about her looks. Physical looks are important in our society. We are bombarded by beautiful models in ads on television. Why do you think physical beauty is so important in our culture? How does God see beauty?

Love Inspired®

Introducing a brand-new 6-book saga from Love Inspired...

Davis Landing

Nothing is stronger than a family's love

Becoming the makeover candidate in her family's magazine wasn't something Heather Hamilton had planned to do, but she refused to miss a deadline. So the shy auburn editor found herself transformed into a beauty that no one, especially photographer Ethan Danes, could keep their eyes off of....

BUTTERFLY SUMMER
BY ARLENE JAMES

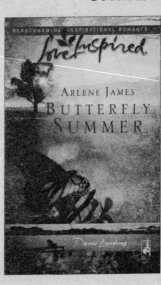

Available July 2006

wherever you buy books.

Steeple Hill®

LIBS

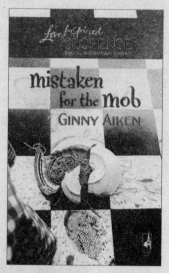

2 Love Inspired novels and a mystery gift... Absolutely FREE!

Visit

www.LoveInspiredBooks.com

for your two FREE books, sent directly to you!

BONUS: Choose between regular print or our NEW larger print format!

There's no catch! You're under no obligation to buy anything. We charge nothing—ZERO—for your first shipment. And you don't have to make any minimum number of purchases.

You'll like the convenience of home delivery at our special discount prices, and you'll love your free subscription to Steeple Hill News, our members-only newsletter.

We hope that after receiving your free books, you'll want to remain a subscriber. But the choice is yours—to continue or cancel, anytime at all! So why not take us up on our invitation, with no risk of any kind!

Love Inspired®
SUSPENSE

TITLES AVAILABLE NEXT MONTH

Don't miss these two stories in July

UNDER SUSPICION by Hannah Alexander
Part of the HIDEAWAY miniseries

When her senator father was murdered, Shona Tremaine became the prime suspect—until an attempt was made on her life. As she worked with her estranged husband, Geoff, to solve the tragic mystery, would their renewed commitment be enough to save Shona's life?

MISTAKEN FOR THE MOB by Ginny Aiken
Being mistaken for a gangster and accused of murders she didn't commit turned librarian Maryanne Wellborn's life on its end. And when serious but handsome FBI agent J. Z. Prophet took the case, she could tell he was determined to bring her down. But when the *real* mob got involved, the situation turned deadly....

LISCNM0606